DREAMS IN THE MIST

Loyalist House
Season I

BARBARA NATTRESS

Order this book online at www.trafford.com
or email orders@trafford.com

Most Trafford titles are also available at major online book retailers.

Printed in the United States of America.

ISBN: 978-1-4669-4939-3 (sc)
ISBN: 978-1-4669-4941-6 (hc)
ISBN: 978-1-4669-4940-9 (e)

Library of Congress Control Number: 2012913203

Trafford rev. 07/24/2012

 www.trafford.com

North America & international
toll-free: 1 888 232 4444 (USA & Canada)
fax: 812 355 4082

For my family

AUTHOR'S NOTES

While owning and operating Windsong Bed and Breakfast for eight years, I always said that someday I would write about the experience. As the bicentennial year of the war of 1812 approached, the time seemed right to tell my story. My ancestors who fought in the war after landing in the area as refugees in 1778 seemed like the perfect family to inhabit Loyalist House B&B.

Of course, the war of 1812 really happened and the circumstances the families endured during this period were dreadful. I have certainly embellished the situation of the Van Every family in this story but have tried to keep historical details accurate.

As this is a work of fiction, the characters in this story are either a figment of my imagination or are used fictitiously.

I hope you enjoy this story about following your passion as well as try some B&B recipes included in the last chapter.

ACKNOWLEDGMENTS

Thank you to my husband for helping run the B&B, especially when I went out of town for several days and left him with all the chores. I also counted on his encouragement to keep writing. You do make the best coffee.

I am indebted to John McCrae for writing the Van Every Story, telling the history of our ancestors. Thank you for being so diligent about the genealogy.

Thank you also to our daughter and my colleague, Christa, for their computer advice.

I am grateful for having such good friends who fueled my imagination with their stories of ghostly experiences.

Thank you to my friends and colleagues who willingly read my manuscript and encouraged me to complete it.

Not to be forgotten are all the special guests who stayed with us at Windsong B&B. Without you, there would be no story. Thank you.

CONTENTS

JUNE

Once again, the river was obscured by fog, and it was now too dark to see the shore or anything on the river. It may have been the wind, but a distinct weeping sound seemed to drift from the house nearby, where a silhouette of a woman dressed in a long white gown could be seen standing at the front steps. Suddenly, there was a slapping noise on the river, and the form of a boat rowing away from the dock was visible for just a moment before it disappeared.

Marilee awoke with a start. It was the same dream she had been having for the past year. Why did this dream continue to haunt her? She decided it was the end-of-the-year stress of her job. Retiring was really the right thing to do. Even though it was 5:00 a.m., she decided to get up and get ready for her very last day of teaching at the school.

"The Bed and Breakfast will be my new passion, and I hope you all will be able to come and stay at Loyalist House," Marilee finished her short speech at the last staff meeting. Many of her colleagues were surprised at her new career choice but were very interested in the idea of a weekend getaway to a B&B in wine country.

The questions afterward ranged from *why would you do this? What are your prices? Do you give discounts to friends?* Marilee had business cards ready to hand out to those who seemed interested and made sure her friends in the history department all had one each.

Marilee Adams had taught for the past twenty years at the local high school. She had enjoyed the students and especially the subjects.

Her favorites were foods and nutrition and fashion design, which allowed creativity and practicality to be incorporated into the lessons. Her students loved her classes for the most part and were quite sad to see her leave, but Marilee realized some of the passion for teaching had gone, and so it was time for a change. Since both Marilee and her husband's children were now married and safely ensconced in their own jobs and lives, being around for children was no longer a necessity.

The idea of running a B&B had been intriguing both to Marilee and her husband, Phillip, for some time, and they had spent a year researching areas suitable for this type of venture. There were many visits to towns in various parts of the country, and, of course, there was always a night's stay in a local B&B as the final test. Checking out the tourist aspects of the area and climate were also important. It took over a year to decide, but they finally chose Niagara Wine Country because of its infrastructure for tourists, its ready-made wine industry, its moderate climate, and its rich historical background. Now, of course, the next big challenge was to find the perfect house for their business. Phillip was an accountant and planned to continue his independent accounting business while helping with the B&B. Both Marilee and Phillip had in their minds what features they wanted in a house, and they knew they might not find everything they wanted.

Phillip was a wiz on the computer and, after consulting a real estate website, had found four homes that might possibly be perfect for their new endeavor. Arrangements were made with an agent to view the houses the next day. Marilee also made reservations at a B&B in the historic part of town as she thought it would be interesting to sample some breakfasts and see how others decorated their guest rooms. She had lots of decorating ideas, but it never hurt to check out the competition.

Armed with listings and maps, Phillip and Marilee set out early Friday to look at homes in the wine region. They arrived in the town of Newbrook midmorning and met with Jack, the realtor, at his office. He was in his mid-forties, dressed casually, and seemed fairly laid-back, at least for the moment. He had made appointments to see six homes that day, so off they went in his car.

Driving through the town was like going back in history. The homes were large older wooden frame homes, with well-kept lawns and amazing gardens. It looked as though homeownership and gardening were competitive sports in this town. Most of the homes were very traditional in design, with architectural details from the 1800s. Dental moldings, leaded glass transoms over doors, and a perfect Georgian balance seemed to be everywhere. The nice feature about this town was that even though the houses displayed similar details, no two homes were the same. There was no evidence of this being a place with cookie-cutter style subdivisions.

Jack mentioned that the majority of the houses in town had been built after 1813 as the Americans, on their departure, had burned the town after being defeated by the British. Only a few homes in the country, away from the lake and the river, had survived. The town had originally been settled in the late 1700s by those remaining loyal to England during the American Revolutionary War. The town had prospered again in the late 1800s as many wealthy industrialists came from Northern United States to build large summer homes. These homes had been well-kept and restored by their owners over the years, and some were now being used as B&B's or inns.

Merilee was delighted to hear that three of the homes they were viewing today were historic homes. She loved the aspect of the historic background, and already, she was planning historic colors and where she would put some of the antique furniture in a new home. She was abruptly brought back to reality as they arrived at the first house.

There were no horse-drawn carriages beside the house, no stables at the rear, no attic windows that might hold secrets, only a white stucco 1930s Arts-and-Crafts style home, with a large SUV in front. What a disappointment—and no road appeal. Jack seemed to read her mind and said that even though this house seemed small, it did have some charming features inside and in the backyard. This house was at the lower end of their price range, so even though Marilee and Phillip were skeptical, they decided to view it anyway.

The house had a lovely front porch and an interesting front door that suddenly appeared to grow taller as you approached. Upon entering, it became apparent that this was a grand small home. The hall, living room, and den all had fifteen-foot ceilings. The walls and coffered ceiling were all wood-paneled in dark-mahogany. The beams and wainscoting projected the look of a private club. It would not have surprised Marilee to see gentlemen smoking cigars and drinking brandy in front of the fireplace. The bathrooms and kitchens had been renovated, and all had the requisite travertine floors, glass and marble showers, and granite countertops. These owners had done their homework before renovating.

Going from the front of the house to the back into the yard was a bit like time travel as you passed through several centuries into a modern twenty-first-century backyard, complete with a pool, a patio, an outdoor kitchen, and an abundance of flowers.

Upstairs, the four bedrooms had been spruced up with paint and accessories but were small and dark. This is where the future work needed to be done. It was a lovely house, but Marilee and Phillip knew it did not really have all the features they desired for their new endeavor. They told Jack this, and he laughed and said that everyone has a list of ten things they want in a house, and the only way to get that is to build it yourself. He did agree with them that the layout of the house was probably not the right one for a B&B.

The next house they visited was just a short walk down the same street. Surrounded by large chestnut trees, it was a stately Victorian two-storey house, well-kept, and with beautiful perennial gardens. The gardens appealed to Marilee as she thought they might be easy to maintain, and the yard would be a relaxing place to serve alfresco meals.

Inside, the entrance was a small hall leading upstairs. Marilee noted in her mind that it might be difficult to carry suitcases up this narrow staircase. The centre hall plan had a formal living and dining room off the front hall. The kitchen was at the back of the house and was quite large, with an eating area for the family. Upstairs, there were five small bedrooms, all with en suite baths that had been incorporated into the closets and part of the bedroom space. The showers were very small, and everything seemed to be made for miniature people. Jack mentioned that these days guests wanted their own private bath, so many people had renovated to give each bedroom its own bath at the expense of space.

Marilee and Phillip wondered where the owners' quarters were, and Jack said the basement had been finished to create a comfortable living space. Both Phillip and Marilee knew they did not want to live in a basement as they felt they had passed that stage of their life and needed lots of daylight to survive. The basement stairs exited from the kitchen and led to a well-lit basement bedroom, family room, laundry room, bathroom, and a large storage room. It was professionally finished and bright, but it was still a basement. They decided to keep this house on their list, but it certainly was not exactly what they had hoped for.

The rest of the day was spent looking at three more houses in the older part of town, all on nice, quiet streets and with good features, but each one had some major drawback that Phillip and Marilee felt they did not want to accept as part of their new dream. At 4:00 p.m., they decided to call it a day and see the last house tomorrow. They hoped the owners would still be able to allow a showing then.

Now, it was time to check into the B&B they had reserved and relax a bit. They both hoped it would be a good experience where they could glean new ideas as well as meet new people. This might be the last time Marilee and Phil would be on this side of the welcoming mat for some time.

The B&B was called Wisteria Inn for obvious reasons as a beautiful wisteria tree covered the pergola at the entrance to the home. The perfume was quite noticeable and initiated a sense of something from another era. Marilee did not know why, but the fragrance transported her mind temporarily to a much gentler time period than the present day. She was quickly brought back to reality when the owner opened the door and welcomed them.

Once inside, Marilee immediately saw that the entire place was decorated in a Victorian style. This was not one of her favorite historical periods, and she wondered what it was that made people feel that Victorian meant putting every ornament, accessory, frill, and tassel on display for all to see. All the surfaces were adorned with figurines, books, china dolls, and children's toys. It could have been an antique store. This place would be a nightmare to keep dust free, but the owner obviously took pride in her home as it was spotless.

The owner, Mrs. Hewitt, showed them to the Prince Albert Suite, and even though it was a fairly large room, it seemed quite crowded with all the bric-a-brac. They were asked to fill in a breakfast request form and leave it in the front hall by 8:00 p.m. Mrs. Hewitt reminded them that it was almost happy hour and wine and cheese or tea and cookies would be served in the garden at the back of the house.

Both Phillip and Marilee thought this was a very civilized idea and would let guests get to know each other. They noted this in their book as something to include at their B&B.

They unpacked, freshened up, and made their way to the garden. It truly was another world in the garden, displaying a natural uncluttered and refreshing feel compared to indoors. Several other couples had already arrived, and after introductions, the conversation turned to local sites and activities. Mr. Hewitt poured wine for everyone, all of which was local. He also answered their questions about the wineries, the fruits, and the best wineries to visit. Philip whispered to Marilee that he could get used to this kind of lifestyle as it was almost like being a bartender in a small pub. They also decided they had to visit as many wineries as possible to become knowledgeable for their guests.

Two of the other couples had reservations at the same restaurant as Phillip and Marilee, so they all decided to walk together and arrange for a larger table. The restaurant was very accommodating, and everyone enjoyed a pleasant evening with new friends as well as an excellent meal.

After dinner, Marilee and Phillip excused themselves from the group and took a short walk around town to go past the homes they had seen and to get an evening view of the one they would see tomorrow.

Back at the B&B, tired but with a million ideas running through their heads, Phillip and Marilee decided to call it an evening and retire to their room to try and unwind. The bed was comfy, with luxuriously high thread count sheets. The bathroom towels were very fluffy and soft, and there were elegant bath products for guest use.

Marilee made her final notes in her ideas book and decided to read for a while. She drifted off to sleep but was transported to another time and place, where there were a lot of unfamiliar faces and homes she seemed to be visiting. She was writing an inventory of furniture and household goods, but there seemed to be no end in sight to the list. All of a sudden, it was light out, and when she looked at the clock, it was almost 8:00 a.m. Phillip was already up and had been out for a walk. She had not even heard him leave the room. She now had to rush to get ready for their eight-thirty breakfast. The dreams she had had during the night were coming back to her only in bits and pieces. Never before had she ever had so many dreams like this, and she wondered if it was because of the atmosphere of the town or the historic inn where they were staying. Anyway, she felt she must not think of it now as she had a busy day ahead of her.

Breakfast was served in the dining room, and as it was a seven-room inn, there were seven tables for two, set up around the room. The tables were nicely appointed, fit for royalty, with all the silver cutlery and crystal glassware that anyone would ever need. Some of the guests had dined earlier, while others were just arriving for the eight-thirty sitting. It was difficult to talk to other guests at breakfast as the location of the tables prevented much conversation. Marilee made a mental note to herself to try and have everyone seated at one table with more family type service that would encourage friendship. The breakfast was delicious with freshly squeezed orange juice, poached pears with pecans, very light, fluffy scones, and freshly baked muffins. The entree was a vegetable frittata served with heritage tomatoes on an endive leaf. An assortment of teas and coffee made it a grand breakfast. At the end of the meal, Mrs. Hewitt brought a small basket that contained the recipes on cards for the guests to take home with them as well as the leftover scones and muffins, in small bags, ready to take as a snack, even though no one felt they would ever eat again. There would be no need for lunch today.

Phillip and Marilee were to meet Jack at his office at 10:00 a.m., so after breakfast, they had just enough time to gather their notes and walk to the office. The idea of walking to everywhere in town appealed to Marilee. Phillip thought the idea of saving gas and wear and tear on the cars and maybe even selling one of the cars was a very positive reason for living in town. They both felt that if they ate what they would serve their guests, they would need to do a lot of walking to stay trim and fit. Giving away the leftovers seemed like a way to keep trim as well.

The office was busy with agents coming in and meeting clients, setting up appointments, and checking the new listings in the area. There seemed to be a lot of people interested in moving to the area and purchasing homes. Marilee hoped that not all these potential buyers were thinking of starting a B&B here in town.

Jack had confirmed the listing in town they had not seen the previous day, and later, they would go to a large home along the river that had only been on the market for two days. The first house was very nice, pleasant inside, tastefully decorated but just not the layout that would allow private spaces for a B&B owner. This was so discouraging that Marilee and Phillip wondered if they ought to buy a lot and build the house the way they wanted it. Jack laughed and said everyone wanted to try that, but there were not many lots in town, and the cost of building had escalated so much that, by completion, the cost would greatly exceed a resale home. Once again, he mentioned they were going to be swept away by the next house along the river.

The drive along the river was unique as it passed vineyards, fruit farms, large new homes, and grand historic homes. Once this had been an Indian trail and a path for marching soldiers, now it was a wonderful spot to picnic and enjoy the view. The river was a winding old river that, over the years, had carved a deep gorge in the limestone rock. At the curves, rapids boiled and churned, while other stretches meandered along to the lake. Fishing boats could be seen floating, waiting for nibbles.

Every so often, a large historic house would appear on the horizon, giving a hint of the history of the area. Jack explained that the area had been settled in by Loyalists, once refugees, who were deeded land around 1782. The Loyalists had realized they could not return to their homes in the United States, so they had decided to stay in this developing territory. Many had become farmers, producing crops to feed their own families and others' in the growing area. Jack told them that his ancestors had settled here but sold their property in the early 1800s as the area had become too populated for their liking.

He continued telling them how this peaceful farming community would be involved in battles against the Americans in the next thirty years that would again destroy homes and lives. Some of the homes this far away from the town had been spared being burned at the end of the war of 1812 but not many remained. The home they were about to view was one of these rare gems. It had been lovingly restored over the years and kept true to the period, with a few modern conveniences, of course.

The home was a large colonial-style home, painted white, with a balanced Georgian exterior. Around the eves was a large dental molding that gave the home an air of grandeur. The pathway leading from the gravel driveway to the front door was edged in reclaimed brick, and on each side of the steps was a garden. At the height of the summer, the Shasta daisies, black-eyed Susans, and colorful annuals bloomed brightly and cheerfully against the lush, green lawn. The house was set back from the river road, almost hidden by the big, old trees. These trees would have many stories to tell if they could talk, but they stood there, providing shade for anyone caring to sit and daydream in the chairs scattered about.

Five steps led up to a small porch with a Grecian-style portico to protect visitors from the elements. The large front door was painted a welcoming yellow, with a brass pineapple knocker in the centre. Another realtor welcomed them to the house and explained that as no guests had checked in for the weekend, they would be able to view the entire house.

The front foyer was very spacious with lots of room for guests carrying suitcases. It was a typical centre hall colonial plan with a dining room on one side and a living room on the other. Stairs further along the hall led to the upstairs. The walls were decorated in a combination of wallpaper and a coordinating paint color that resembled caramel with a touch of sage. The mood of the entrance created a relaxing feeling as soon as one entered the hall.

At the back of the house, there was a kitchen and a family room, used by the owners. The kitchen had been updated and had the requisite granite counter tops, professional gas range, subzero refrigerator, and two dishwashers—all the items people wanted in a home these days. This kitchen would be a dream to cook in. The corner near the door had an interesting half door in the wall, and the agent explained that it was a dumbwaiter that carried food from the original kitchen in the lower level up to the dining area. Originally built in 1782, the house had been rebuilt in 1817 and then several additions had been added over the years. The original owners had had slaves who had cared for the family, cooking, cleaning, and working the land. The dumbwaiter apparently went all the way to the attic and was used to transport laundry within the house. It was actually big enough to carry a queen-size mattress.

Marilee and Phillip asked if the history of the house was written down anywhere as it would be interesting to have it for guests to read while visiting and for promotional purposes of the B&B. They were assured by their agent that it was all documented in the local museum as well as by the owners.

They continued on to see the upper levels and had their choice of using the front staircase near the entrance or back staircase from the kitchen. This would work really well for a B&B as you could easily get to the kitchen in the morning without disturbing guests.

Upstairs, there were six bedrooms, five at the front and one in the private space at the back. Each room had its own en suite bathroom, making it perfect for a Bed and Breakfast. The owner's suite at the back was attached to a sitting room, an office, and the laundry room. This part of the house had been an addition to the original home built in the seventy's.

Each of the five bedrooms had been decorated with a nature theme in mind. The colors were muted but lively enough to give the rooms a bright and cheery feeling. There was no Victorian whimsy anywhere, thank goodness. The home was so well cared for and loved that Marilee wondered why the owners were selling. Their agent explained that they had been running a B&B for ten years and wanted to retire. He mentioned that the average time people ran their homes as B&B's was three to five years as most were older when they had started the job. These owners were in their seventies and wanted more free time. They were also willing to sell most of the furnishings in the home and had a list of linens and equipment included with the sale.

Marilee and Phillip continued looking at the upper level, the attic, and the basement, checking out all the working parts of the home. The property behind the house led down to the river where there was a carriage house, a boathouse, a dock, several small boats, and other water equipment. This was all included in the sale of the home. Beside the dock was a sitting area with comfy looking chairs and a spectacular view both up and down the river. Across the river was New York State where many large homes were situated along the river. They looked about the same vintage as the ones on the Canadian side, and it all looked very peaceful. Marilee and Phillip were both thinking about the period two hundred years ago, when this area had been involved in a war and was not so peaceful.

As they walked back to the main house, they both commented that this was exactly what they were looking for as it could be a business as well as a family home where they could enjoy the next stage of their lives. They decided to think about it overnight and make the final decision and arrangements in the morning. This had been an exciting day, and there were so many thoughts rolling around in their heads that they needed to find a quiet spot to sort it all out. That night over dinner, they decided it was the right choice to put an offer on the house and try to close and be moved in before the summer season ended.

The next day, the offer was written up, presented, negotiated several times, and finally accepted by late evening. Phillip and Marilee were so excited they couldn't possibly think of sleeping, so they decided a walk around town would have a calming effect on them.

At night, the town had a completely different atmosphere. The leaves on the trees were very thick, hiding the streetlights and casting eerie shadows around the buildings. The clip-clop sound of the horse and carriage easily transported one's imagination back to an era when the town had been built. This had been the centre for the developing country side and, at one time, the capital of Upper Canada. Before that, it had been the gathering point for settlers loyal to the British Monarchy who were trying to escape persecution and death by the newly independent American States. These Loyalists had quickly left all their possessions behind and found a safe haven in a part of the country still belonging to England. As tradespersons and shopkeepers, walking through forests and wilderness had been a new and difficult experience for them. When they had arrived at their destination, in order to survive, the land had to be cleared, shelters built, and food grown and harvested. As in any refugee camp, disease often had often taken its toll, especially among the young and the elderly.

Marilee and Phillip both enjoyed history and were quite excited about learning more stories relating to the settlement of the town. As they walked along the streets, the houses seemed to be waiting to tell their stories of love, wonderful family events, business dealings, and tragedies. That would all have to wait as they had returned to the B&B and were now ready to call it a night. Tomorrow, they would start their new journey.

They had just thirty days to pack their own household goods, purchase all the necessary things for a B&B, move, and unpack to be ready for their guests, who would be arriving just ten days after the move. Of course, there were also all the good-bye parties to attend in their old community. Needless to say, the time went by very quickly, and Phillip and Marilee felt as though they were on a treadmill on which the speed just kept increasing.

JULY

Finally, moving day arrived, everything went as planned, nothing was lost, and by 10:00 p.m., Phillip and Marilee had become the fourth owners of a grand home now to be known as Loyalist House B&B. Although the house was in total disarray, they both fell into bed and slept soundly the first night in their new home.

The next morning, a basket of goodies was found at their front door. It had all the essentials, a carafe of coffee, mugs, muffins, scones, homemade jam, and plates and cutlery. There was a note welcoming them to the area and was signed by the neighbor to the south. This was a lovely surprise as the coffee pot and breakfast fixings were still packed in a box somewhere in the house among all the other cartons.

The first day in their new home was spent unpacking, arranging for services to be connected, and trying to find places for all their things. The kind neighbor returned at noon to collect her basket and exchanged it for a lunch basket. This was beyond the welcoming that Phillip and Marilee had ever imagined, and they appreciated it very much. She introduced herself as Jeannie Hazelton and insisted they call her Jeannie as she would probably not respond to Mrs. Hazelton as that was her mother-in-law. Jeannie looked as though she would be a lot of fun at a party, had a flamboyant fashion sense, and talked a mile a minute. She was a wealth of information about people and places in the area and left her phone number to call if they ever needed anything. As fast as she had appeared, she left in her convertible, blonde hair blowing in the wind.

By evening, things were somewhat organized, and the kitchen was all set to go. A dinner of take-out food and a bottle of local wine were enjoyed on the back patio that looked up and down the river. They decided not to do any more unpacking that night as they were too tired.

Marilee was just drifting off to sleep when she heard the familiar sobbing sound of the haunting dream. She was now awake, or so she thought, but she could still hear it. As she tiptoed out the bedroom door and down the hall, she noticed the window had been left open in one of the bedrooms. The curtains were fluttering in the breeze, and the sound was louder. As she walked to the window, the sobbing stopped. This room overlooked the river, and the moon was reflecting on the water. She thought this was odd as before, this scene was only in a dream, but now, it seemed a bit more real. She closed the window, decided it was the wind and her extreme tiredness, and went back to bed.

The next morning was bright and sunny, and both Phillip and Marilee got an early start on the unpacking. There were just nine days left before guests would be arriving. The previous owner had continued to book reservation requests before they left, which meant Loyalist House would be fairly busy for the last two months of summer. They had also left many of the furnishings, especially in the B&B area, so it only required a bit of staging for the public side of the house to be ready for guests.

The day finally arrived, and Phillip and Marilee were ready to welcome their first guests to Loyalist House. Marilee checked the rooms for the twentieth time to make sure she hadn't forgotten anything. She had lists for groceries, baking, necessary serving dishes, and just about everything else anyone could think of, and all had been checked many times. Phillip kept checking the computer so he would know the guest's names when they arrived. He also kept checking the driveway so he wouldn't miss a car approaching. Check-in time was to be between 3:00 p.m. and 6:00 p.m., so when the doorbell rang at 4:00 p.m., both Marilee and Phillip had to stop themselves from running to the door. They wondered aloud if they would always be this nervous about guests checking in or whether this was just opening night jitters.

The guests were two couples who were travelling together and had come to attend the cherry festival plus other events in the area. They seemed pleased with their rooms and complimented the interiors. Both Phillip and Marilee found it difficult to treat them as customers rather than friends but had been warned by Jeannie not to cross the line to preserve their privacy. That evening, the two couples went out for dinner and returned about 10:00 p.m. After a short visit in the library, they said good night and retired to their rooms. Marilee and Phillip looked at each other, thinking that this was too easy. They had prepared the food for breakfast as completely as they could, so they decided to go to bed early as they really were quite tired.

At 2:00 a.m., Marilee sat upright in bed, grabbing Phillip and asking if he was awake and if he had heard the noise. Of course he hadn't, but now, he could hear the creaking above them in the attic. It sounded like someone was walking around up there. It continued for a few more minutes and then, as suddenly as it had started, it stopped.

They realized they had been barely breathing and let out a big sigh. They figured it couldn't be the guests as there was no access to the attic from the guest area. If it was someone, how did they get there? Grabbing a flashlight and a candlestick as a weapon, Phillip decided to go up to the attic. Marilee picked up her cell phone and followed him. There were lights in the attic, so it was easy to see, and since they had not moved anything up there yet, the entire area was empty, with no uninvited guests lurking about. It was a mystery, but it would have to be solved at a later time. They both went back to bed and decided not to mention it unless the guests brought up the subject at breakfast. Maybe it could be explained as large squirrels if anyone asked. Neither of them slept a wink for the rest of the night.

Daylight finally arrived, and Phillip and Marilee got up to prepare breakfast for their guests. After a sleepless night, they were both very tired but somewhat keyed up as this was their first breakfast for the guests. The prep went well, and everything was ready in the dining room when the guests came downstairs. The day promised to be sunny and warm, so everyone was in a cheerful mood and ready for a day of exploring the area. The fresh fruit, scones, muffins, and the frittata were all eaten with gusto, with no leftovers in sight. Phillip and Marilee joined their guests on the porch for coffee and enjoyed discovering a bit about them and where they were from. They answered questions about the area and attractions that were worth a visit. The topic of the noise in the night did not enter the conversation—thankfully. The guests left for the day, and Phillip and Marilee began the tasks of cleaning, primping the rooms, and starting the prep for the next day. These guests were staying over again, and another guest would be arriving later in the day, so they would have three rooms filled tonight.

The remainder of the day was filled with washing, ironing, grocery shopping, and answering requests for rooms, and before Marilee knew it, the doorbell rang. It was her next guests, arriving for the evening. The day had passed so quickly that there had not been time to sit down or chat with Phillip about the noise in the attic. Phillip had spent the day outside, unpacking things in the carriage house and working in the yard. All the guests were settled in their rooms, so Phillip and Marilee decided it was time to sit on the back patio, with a glass of wine before dinner. As they had the same guests for one more day, they figured that tomorrow would be a good time to go up to the attic to see if there were any holes needing repair, to keep critters out. There were also some old trunks Phillip had found in the carriage house that could be stored up there for now.

The next day, after breakfast, Phillip carried the two trunks up to the attic. They were not too large and not overly heavy, but the locks on the front were somewhat rusted and could not be opened. After Marilee had cleaned the rooms and had the laundry going, she joined him in the attic. Together, they walked all around the perimeter of the attic, looking for holes that squirrels might enter from, but none could be seen. While surveying the space, it was decided that shelves could be erected to hold some unused and seldom-used items like suitcases and boxes of books. It was a very dry attic, and as the house was well-insulated, it did not become overheated in the summer. The one interesting feature in the attic was a window at the back of the house.

It was an oval shape and faced the river, and even though it needed a good cleaning, you could see for quite a distance up and down the river. It was also a good spot to view the large houses on the United States side of the river. Marilee thought this might even make a great spot to create a small getaway where she could read or nap, if there ever was any time to do that.

It was the beginning of peach season, so Marilee drove to one of the local fruit stands to buy fresh tree-ripened peaches as she had planned to make peach French toast the next morning. The peaches were large and juicy this year and would be great as a topping for the French toast. While there, she met her neighbor, who told her about an upcoming lecture at the museum. An historian from the area would be speaking about family life when the Loyalists had been settling in the area. Marilee thought this would be interesting, so they arranged to go together.

The next morning, the recipe for the French toast was a hit, and everyone asked if Marilee would share it with them. She had anticipated this question and had all her recipes on the computer, so it was quite easy to print off the needed copies. All the guests checked out that morning, and the house would be empty until the weekend. That weekend, all five rooms were booked for three consecutive nights. So far, they had been as busy as they wanted to be, but of course, it was just their first week. That weekend would be the test to see if fully booked was as good as it sounded.

amazing that any evidence actually remained about life at that time. How had people had the time or energy to keep track of all that was going on? And had it not taken every waking moment just to keep oneself alive?

Mr. Russell was to be here at the museum for two days, doing some research on the war and going over some new articles that had been found recently in a home in the area. Marilee asked him how he had found new material in homes, considering this was such an historic area but built after 1814. The papers he was researching had recently been found in the walls of a house being renovated. It was on the outskirts of town and had escaped the fire. Marilee began to think of the trunks found in the carriage house and decided she would try and open them soon to see if there was anything interesting. She decided not to mention this to Mr. Russell, but she knew she had his address if she needed to contact him.

Right now, she had to get to the grocery store, buy food, go home, and begin preparing for the next guests coming in tonight. She was pleased that today she had taken the time to learn more about the area, and now her interest was piqued about the house they had purchased.

SEPTEMBER

September arrived, and Marilee and Phillip thought things might slow down a bit so they could take in some of the tourist spots their guests were talking about. This was not to be. It seemed that in September, all those people who did not want to travel in the heat of summer or when everyone else traveled, decided to come to the area. Bookings were coming in fast and furious along with some that had been booked by the previous owners. They were soon fully booked every weekend and at least three or four week days as well. This, of course, was grape harvest time, so people were coming for a different reason. Who could resist tasting all the various wines at the numerous wineries in the area? Marilee and Phillip decided that if they were to enjoy Thanksgiving weekend with their family, they would have to close off bookings now, or their families might have to stay elsewhere. This was the kind of job where you had to control it, or it would soon control you. They had met some other B&B owners who were exhausted by the time September rolled around as they had taken no days off since April. They both decided this would not be their lifestyle. This was supposed to be retirement and enjoyable, after all.

Fall was a great season. Many groups began to meet again, the weather was perfect for eating outdoors, and people visiting were still happy to be on vacation and wanted to enjoy their visit.

Marilee's neighbor Jeannie came for a visit one day and wanted Marilee to help at the museum. They needed volunteers to assist with school programs as well as set up new displays. Marilee's teaching background would be perfect for a volunteer. The museum had a wonderful reputation for its school programs, offering curriculum enrichment classes from historic clothing to reenacting the historic battles fought in the area. Apparently, teachers had to book well in advance to be able to bring their classes on a field trip.

Marilee went for an interview, and several days later, she was hired as an historic interpreter for the school program. She figured winter would be a slower time with the B&B, so this would fit in quite nicely. She was also excited about learning more about the local history.

One September weekend, Loyalist House was fully booked, and Marilee and Phillip were ready, as usual, to welcome their guests. Four couples checked in, and all were thrilled to be spending the weekend in wine country. Shortly after seven, the phone rang, and it was the fifth couple saying they had been delayed in traffic and would not be there until about nine. Phillip said not to worry; he would hold their room for them. Ten o'clock arrived, and the guests had not arrived. By eleven, Phillip and Marilee decided to go to bed but leave the lights on and the door locked. They would hear the door bell. Phillip awoke suddenly at one-thirty and noticed the lights were still on. The guests had still not arrived. Phillip decided they would not show, so he went downstairs and turned off all the lights. Two hours later, the door bell rang, and there at the door, stood a young man and his wife with their luggage. They proceeded to tell Phillip that the illumination of the falls which always took place at nine had been delayed until after midnight due to problems. This story seemed very farfetched, but Phillip quietly showed them to their room and said that breakfast was at nine and checkout was at eleven. He just hoped that no one else in the house was disturbed by their entry.

The next morning at breakfast, everyone but the late-entry couple were on time. Marilee decided to start without them as it wasn't fair to the rest to make them wait. Finally, the couple arrived, somewhat surprised that they would have to take their places at the same table with the other guests. They had only booked in for the one night, and partway through breakfast, they suggested to Phillip that he could book them in for another night. Phillip had overheard part of a conversation at the table about them being at the casino last night and decided he didn't want to repeat the late night wait, so he said they were fully booked for the night. The guests seemed nonplussed and then suggested that Phillip go online and book them a place for the night. At that point, Phillip was ready to explode but politely said he did not have time to do that for them. When he returned to the kitchen, Marilee knew something was wrong. He told her what had transpired, and Marilee decided she needed to keep a list of guests who might not be welcome back at Loyalist House, and this couple would be first on the list. Some people really didn't understand how a B&B was run and should just stay in hotels instead.

The rest of the morning went well, and all the guests who were staying another night were lovely, considerate, and would be welcome back anytime.

Jeannie called Marilee the next day and said the museum needed her as an interpreter for three days next week as there were school groups booked. This would be interesting as Marilee had guests booked in for some of those days. She would just have to figure out if the times would overlap and if Phillip might like to be in charge of the latter part of breakfast. At lunch, she filled Phillip in on the scheduling conflicts and asked if he might be interested in finishing up breakfast on two mornings next week. He thought that he could handle that if all the baking was done ahead of time. Phillip thought he might be able to do the laundry as well. Marilee just smiled.

Early Tuesday morning, Marilee was up making sure all the breakfast preparations had been completed so it would be easy for Phillip to make breakfast. Fortunately, the guests were staying two days, so the rooms would just need tidying up after breakfast. Marilee was dressed in her pioneer costume, so she was ready to begin teaching the program once she arrived at the museum. She was wearing a cotton print dress with long sleeves and a round collar, an apron over the skirt, and a mop cap on her head. She had her shawl ready to go with her basket at the front door. When the guests came down for breakfast, they were somewhat taken aback at the sight of a pioneer woman in the modern dining room. Marilee explained to them what she was doing and why she was dressed as a pioneer. They all thought the museum might be a good place to visit while they were there.

Marilee arrived at the museum and quickly found out where she was working and what she would be teaching. Today, she was introducing a grade four class to simple machines in pioneer homes that incorporated gears and pulleys. The museum was fortunate enough to have the space to set up replicas of rooms in homes dating from early 1800 to 1870.

All the antique pieces of equipment were on the table in the kitchen of one of the 1860s era homes. It would be fun to ask what the class thought the piece of equipment was and what made it work. When her class arrived, they were quite noisy and full of energy, but they quickly became interested in the program and very curious about the equipment. They all had ideas about its use, but most of the answers were far from the right one. The morning flew by, and it was lunch time, with two more classes coming in the afternoon. Some classes were more interested than others, and one class in particular seemed to be in another world all together. Maybe it was the time of day or maybe this one class had not done any preparation about the subject beforehand. It was interesting to see how different kids were.

The next day, Marilee returned to the museum, still dressed as a pioneer, but this time, she was helping a grade two class understand where pioneers had purchased some of the things they had needed but couldn't make themselves. The museum had a room set up as a general store, stocked with articles that might have been for sale in the 1860s. Today, they would be learning about bartering, paying bills, sending letters, and how long it took for goods to be delivered once they were ordered. The classes were always amazed at the simple toys which had been available to children—but only if their parents had had the money. It was also fun for them to know the cost of things in 1860 compared with today. The classes today had been studying pioneers in their school and knew lots of answers and had many good questions to ask. This class was really fun for Marilee to work with.

The next day was a repeat of the first day, except, as with people, things were never the same and did not always have the same outcome.

Marilee decided this would be a fun way to spend her spare time in the winter.

Phillip, on the other hand, was not so sure that running the B&B was his thing. He enjoyed helping out at breakfast, keeping the accounts, and preparing the promotional materials, but doing dishes, cleaning bathrooms, and doing the laundry were really not his idea of retirement. Of course, most of Marilee's museum work would be in the winter when they would have no B&B guests. He guessed he could survive the few days he was needed.

September continued with guests every week and with Marilee spending a fair amount of time at the museum. This was almost like working full-time.

OCTOBER

Before she knew it, September was over, and Thanksgiving celebrations were quickly approaching. Their family had not been to visit since they had moved, and everyone was excited to see the new place and stay in a B&B for free. Marilee joked that it might be "Bed and get-your-own Breakfast" for family members. But, of course, that wouldn't happen as she wanted to try some new recipes on the family to get their opinions. Her big job before they came would be to childproof a couple of rooms where the grandchildren would be sleeping. She thought the attic room would be a great place for them to play as there was nothing there to worry about. Now she just had to find the box of toys she had been saving all these years for this moment.

The toys were in the carriage house, and even though Marilee had thought they were in good shape, they looked a bit tired after all these years. Maybe she should go and try to find new ones for the children when they came. She decided against it, washed them, and took them to the attic. The front side of the room would be a perfect place to put down the foam blocks and all the toys. A short table was installed as a place to color, and some cushions on the floor made a perfect spot to read. The attic was looking more livable than ever. The two trunks were stacked at the far end of the large room, and Marilee thought that now might be a good time to investigate the contents. She went over to lift the top trunk off but found it was too heavy for her, so she decided to just open it where it was. She remembered that the trunks were locked and found a pin and a nail she was removing from the room for safety reasons. Neither worked. She would have to either break the lock or find a locksmith to help her. She decided on the locksmith as damaging the lock would lower the value of the antique trunk. This project would have to wait until another time. She would call Jeannie to help her find a locksmith.

The next few days, she de-cluttered the bedrooms of anything breakable and made up the rooms for the family. The weather man was promising a beautiful weekend, so the outside also was getting a cleaning. Friday finally arrived, and by late afternoon, everyone was settled in and ready for supper. Her oldest daughter and husband had two boys aged three and five, while her youngest daughter and husband had an eighteen-month-old daughter. The two boys thought it was great to run up the front stairs and down the back to the kitchen. *They should sleep well tonight after all that exercise.*

Everyone had lots to talk about, and after the children were all asleep, the three couples sat in the front room, chatting about what was happening in their lives. Phillip had found some local wines he wanted everyone to try, and before they knew it, the grandfather clock struck twelve.

Marilee finished up a few things in the kitchen, and all was quiet in the house. She was just about to fall asleep, or so she thought, when she heard a noise in the attic. Surely no one had gone up there? She thought about getting up to go and check, but soon, the soft weeping began again. Was it the wind or was it the wine she had drunk that was doing this? At this point, Marilee noticed she was standing by the river and looking back at a house that looked familiar. The sobbing noise had stopped, but now, the loud voices of men arguing could be heard.

Arguments

Two men and three boys were standing in two groups. The men were arguing about loyalties. The one was saying it was wrong of the Americans to just decide they could take their land, especially after basically chasing them from their homes a few years earlier. The other said they may as well all be one country and join together to fight against the French and the British. The argument went back and forth, leaving the young boys feeling uncomfortable. They had been playing together before the men had arrived, but both the fathers had made sure the boys were separated, and the playing stopped. These boys had grown up together, but now it seemed they were not allowed to be together.

A young man wandered toward the two groups. He had a faraway but happy smile on his face. Peter was the son of one of the fathers and was actually working for the other on this farm. He was also smitten with Mr. Van Every's oldest daughter, Hannah, and most days, he had a chance to talk to her. He had been invited to several parties at the Van Every home but was always accompanied by his parents. He was pretty sure Hannah liked him, and they did manage, several times, to sneak down to the river and talk about how some day they might marry. They knew they would have to wait until Hannah was several years older and had finished her education. Peter considered himself an adult as he was sixteen.

All of a sudden, Peter's father angrily told his sons, including Peter, to come along with him and that he would not be working at the Van Every's farm any more. Peter was stunned, and even though he did not know the reason, he did as his Father said and followed. The Gillham family lived just down the river from the Van Every's, and often, it was easier to go between the two farms by paddling on the river rather than over land. Today, they returned to their farm by boat.

John Gillham was a proud, hardworking man who had moved to the area after the Revolutionary War. He felt no animosity toward those who had left before or during the war, but neither did he feel the two countries should be so politically opposed. Being one country would make more sense, and he did not see Van Every's point of view about remaining loyal to Britain. Now, it seemed there was going to be another war about this exact topic. It could only lead to hardships, food shortages, and possibly moving his family to a safer spot once again. He must get home quickly and begin to look for a safer place to live.

He had heard about land on the other side of the river being for sale and decided that tomorrow he and Peter would go and investigate.

When he arrived home, he informed his wife and three daughters that they should begin packing only the important and valuable items and be ready to move within the week. Peter and his two brothers should gather some food for only the animals that would be taken with them. To get to the others side of the river, it meant crossing at a spot that was not too deep and not moving too swiftly. The animals would have to be able to swim, following the boat and a barge.

Peter was horrified that this was all happening so fast. He wanted to talk to Hannah, but he knew his Father would not allow him to return to their farm. If only he did not have to go with his father to find land, he could possibly get word to Hannah and meet her at their secret hiding place by the river. He decided to wait until they returned from over the river and hoped he would have a few days to see her before the family left.

Peter knew that if they moved, the hired help at their farm would not go with them. That night, when he was supposed to be gathering food for the cows and horses, Peter talked to one of the farmhands he knew he could trust and asked him to take a note to Hannah. He had to hope that this would work as there was no other way.

The next morning, very early, John Gillham and his son Peter set out down the river to the crossing spot to go and look for land. Along the way, Peter was surprised to see soldiers beginning to gather and setting up camp in the town. These must be British soldiers as they were wearing red coats. The soldiers did not seem to pay much attention to them as they crossed the river, and Peter hoped the same would be true when they returned. The land on the other side of the river was just as overgrown and hard to navigate as it was on the Upper Canada side. It was tough going, but after a day and a half, they found their way into a small settlement and began to ask about land for sale.

There was property available up the river toward the rapids, but there was a trail to it along the river. John and Peter went with the official and, after several hours, came to an open spot where they could see the other side. It was hard to tell because of the growth of trees, but John seemed to think he was very near to being across the river from his own property. This was the land for sale. It was a fifty-acre parcel that ran from the river inland. The soil seemed about the same as on his property, and he could build a home away from the river to be safe during this uncertain time.

It took several more days to firm up the deal and another two days to return to their farm in Upper Canada. All that time, Peter had been thinking about whether his friend had managed to get his note to Hannah. He would sneak out after dinner tomorrow and take the boat the short distance up the river to meet Hannah. At that point, he did not know what he would tell her. Should he leave his family and hope the Van Every's would accept him into their family? Should he and Hannah run away and get married? How would they live? Could he stay on the family farm in Upper Canada? If he left, would he ever see his family again?

*   *   *

Saturday morning dawned a beautiful, sunny, crisp fall day. Everyone gathered for breakfast and enjoyed the apple pancakes, fresh cranberry-orange muffins, and coffee. At the table, over their second mugs of coffee, they tried to decide what they would do for the day. Finally, it was decided that the men and the oldest children would tour a local historical monument while the women would take the baby and go to a craft fair. They would all meet back at the house in time to collectively prepare dinner.

Today, at the monument commemorating General Brock, there was a special celebration to mark the anniversary of the Battle of Queenston Heights. The American army had invaded at Queenston in 1812, and while General Brock had rushed his troops to confront the invaders, the battle had ended in favor of the British, but the beloved General had been killed.

There were marching fife and drum bands, a large number of Union Jack flags, and many people dressed as British and American militia. Earlier, there had been a recreation of a battle between the two groups. The fife and drum bands marched to a gathering area, and after a few speeches, all the Loyalists were invited to have a piece of celebratory cake. Of course, almost everyone was recognized as a Loyalist—even those dressed in American militia costumes.

Phillip, his sons-in-law Gary and Allan, and the two boys headed for the car after the ceremonies and decided to stop at a winery on the way home to pick up some local wines for their BBQ tonight. The wineries were in the midst of harvesting grapes, so there was a lot to see as well as some of last year's vintages to taste. The children were impressed with the tractors and other pieces of heavy equipment being used to transport grapes from farmer's fields to the winery for processing. The men were impressed with several of the wines they tasted and had trouble deciding which ones to buy. In the end, they left with a case of a variety of reds and whites. It had been a good day.

The women drove a short distance to the outdoor craft show that Marilee's neighbor had mentioned to her. It was much larger than Marilee had imagined and included an antique sale. They decided to skip the craft section and headed straight to the antiques. The antiques ranged from early European periods to twentieth-century household items. After walking around and looking for about an hour, they decided that if any piece of antiquity wasn't here, it probably did not exist. No one was really interested in furniture, so they concentrated on the accessories available. Several vendors had interesting candle holders that Marilee thought would look nice on the mantle. The pair she decided to purchase was pewter and had a note from the original owner explaining their origin and dates. They all wondered why these had not remained in a family and what circumstances had forced the family to dispose of such lovely items. Her daughters, Janine and Emma, each found a mirror perfect for their homes, and they were ready to walk back to the car to go home when Marilee spied several trunks for sale in one of the vendor's stalls. These looked similar to the ones they had found in the carriage house when they had moved in. She suggested the girls take their purchases and the baby to the car, and she would be along shortly. The vendor was quite willing to talk to her about the history and uses of the trunks. It seemed that this style of trunk was used by Loyalists escaping from the Eastern United States during the Revolutionary War, so it dated back to the early and mid-1700s. It would have been used to carry any small, valuable, and useful items to a new home. Later, they were used as hope chests by young women or for storage of unused clothing items. Marilee asked about the locks and if they could be opened in any way without damaging the lock mechanism. The vendor, Mr. Grey, said he had been collecting keys for many years and had quite a selection, some of which worked on this type of lock. Immediately, Marilee became very excited and couldn't decide whether to buy all his keys or the trunks. Logic prevailed, and instead, she asked where his shop was located. It was in a small town only a half-hour's drive from her house. She told him of the trunks she had inherited with the house and asked if someday he could come with his keys to see if any would work on the trunks' locks. There might not be anything in them that was valuable, but opening them was now becoming an obsession with Marilee. Mr. Grey said he would be delighted to help her and see if the trunks were authentic. A date was set up for the visit, and Marilee hurried back to the car and began to tell Janine and Emma about the trunks in her attic. They all decided to let the men get dinner, and they would go up to see if there was any way they could open them tonight. This had been a good day.

Upon their return to Loyalist House, there was quite a bit of chatter from everyone retelling the adventures of the day. The children were excited about seeing guns being fired, the men had already begun to taste the wines they had purchased, and the women could only talk about what might be in the trunks. Of course, reality happened, and the children suddenly became starved, the baby needed to be fed, so everyone flipped into work mode to get supper ready and the kids to bed and then the adults could spend the evening together.

After dinner, with the children all tucked in bed, no one had the energy to go up to the attic and try to unlock trunks. Instead, the family enjoyed an evening chatting about all the things families talk about on holidays. Marilee and Phillip had several interesting stories about eccentric guests who had stayed with them. Phillip had kept track of the number of guests who were unable to lock and unlock the front door. He figured at least a third had trouble with this simple task and wondered how people coped at home. By the end of the evening,

Phillip had everyone laughing at the funny stories he could tell about running a B&B.

A few plans were made for the next day, and everyone headed off to bed, satisfied that this had been a wonderful day.

The next morning was once again a sunny, crisp fall day, just waiting for adventures to begin. Today, the family would enjoy Thanksgiving dinner together for the first time in this new home. After breakfast, everyone pitched in to help prepare. Even the children helped set the dining room table and worked on crafty turkeys to be used as table decorations. By noon, the aroma of roasting turkey was wafting through the whole house, and everyone was anticipating the big dinner. It was nice to have the whole family visiting, around the house for the day, involved in preparing the meal. The boys spent most of the time running around the yard and trying to see if they could convince their grandfather to get the boat out of the boathouse and go for a ride on the river. Being so late in the season, Phillip did not want to do this, so he convinced them to try fishing from the dock instead. Fishing was fun, and they did get to see several really fast boats go by, so the boys were happy. Dinner that evening was delicious, and everyone went to bed feeling as though they had eaten too much and were ready for a good night's sleep.

The next morning was a busy time packing up all the gear that goes with travelling with children, and the families were ready to leave Loyalist House until Christmas. Both girls mentioned to Marilee that they never did get around to opening the trunks in the attic, but maybe that could happen on the next visit. Marilee privately thought she could never wait over two months to see what they might contain. Goodbyes were said, and the house became quiet once again. The regular chores of cleaning rooms, doing laundry, and getting rooms ready for the next guests took the better part of the afternoon and evening. Turkey sandwiches on the back porch were supper that night, and both Phillip and Marilee were ready to call it a day before midnight. It had been a great first Thanksgiving at Loyalist House B&B.

The Letter

It was a lovely, early summer day, not too hot to be out walking in the garden. The herbs were starting to bloom, and the smell of lavender leaves was very evident as she walked along the pathways. Further along, her mother had planted roses as a reminder of her family home in England. Hannah's Mother had been very homesick when she first came to Canada, and by planting roses that reminded her of England, she had, over the years, become quite happy with her life here. Hannah's family was very well-off compared to many other families in the region, and the fact that they had a garden with flowers just for pleasure was certainly a sign of their wealth. Hannah was daydreaming of her future, with Peter, she hoped, and maybe on a farm like this one. She was suddenly surprised when one of the farmworkers handed her a note while she was walking in the garden. He seemed nervous about handing it to her and nervously looked around to make sure no one was watching. He said he had been given the letter by another worker on the Gillham farm. He quickly left to return to work. Hannah immediately walked down to the river where there was privacy to read the note. She suspected it was from Peter as she had not heard from him or seen him around the farm for the past week. She had also heard her parents talking about some neighbors wanting to be part of the United States. She did not really understand all the details of why so many families were becoming divided, but she did know everyone was on edge these days. She found a chair by the river and opened the letter. It was from Peter, and her heart seemed to skip a few beats as she began to read, but soon, she realized these were not the words she had been hoping for. The letter explained how Peter's father was moving the family across the river next week and how he was expected to go with them. He seemed to have been thinking as he had written, asking Hannah for ideas on what they should do. Peter wanted Hannah to meet him at midnight tonight by the dock in front of her house. He would come by boat and whistle three times when he was close. She should respond by chirping three times like the whip-poor-will. Hannah began to plan her evening thinking that if she borrowed some of her brother's clothes, she would be less likely to be seen. Sneaking out of the house might be tricky, but she knew everyone was usually asleep by midnight. She would just have to go over the path out of the house to see if there were any creaks in the floor to avoid.

*　　*　　*

October was a lovely time of year. It was cool, not as busy as the summer, and along the back roads, there was a distinct wine smell coming from the wineries where grape crushing was taking place. This was the time of year when Marilee felt very lucky to live in this area. Cleaning up the gardens for winter, usually a dreaded job, was enjoyable as the weather was perfect, and the planning for next year was exciting. Plants were moved from one area of the garden to another to create several sitting areas for the guests as well as the family.

The local garden centers were fabulous places to get ideas for fall decorating, with every color and variety of Mum available for the garden. Pumpkins and baskets of fall flowers were purchased to decorate the front of the house as well as the back patio. Just a few ghosts and goblins strategically located on the property was all that was needed to decorate their home for Halloween. Marilee wondered how many trick-or-treaters might come by on Halloween and asked her neighbor Jeannie. She found out that most children stayed in town, where the houses were closer together. Last year, Jeannie had had only five children knock on her door. Marilee was a bit disappointed as she loved to see the younger children all dressed up, and Marilee often dressed up in a costume herself. She still decided she would plan on having treats for more than five children and would give the leftovers to her grandchildren if she and Phillip did not eat them first.

Halloween evening came, and Phillip and Marilee dressed up as Raggedy Ann and Andy and waited for kids to come. At 6:00 p.m., Jeannie brought her two grandchildren, and the rest of the evening was silent. No kids, big or little, came. It was disappointing, but Phillip and Marilee had supper uninterrupted while dressed as rag dolls. Their dessert that night was candy.

The local paper that arrived each Thursday had a list of upcoming events for the next few weeks. As Marilee read the list, she became quite excited about a few of them. One in particular was a day of house tours of homes in the area. Some homes were very old, while others had interesting architectural details. All would be decorated for Christmas. What a chance to peek into some of the houses you pass each day and to get new decorating ideas! She marked that weekend on the calendar and the phone number of where to buy tickets. There were also several concerts in town and events at the museum she wanted to attend. It looked like a busy time until Christmas.

The date with Mr. Grey was finally here. Today, he was coming to look at the two trunks in the attic to see if he had any keys that would fit the locks. He arrived right on time and was as anxious as Marilee to see these trunks. They all picked up a coffee and went up to the attic. Phillip had previously pulled the trunks to the centre of the room, close to the windows so there would be lots of light. Upon examination, Mr. Grey declared that the trunks were of English origin and probably dated back to the mid-1700s. They were in remarkable shape for their age but had obviously been used for travelling as was evident by the bumps and scrapes. Mr. Grey pulled out his great ring of keys and began to sort through them. As he had narrowed down the origin and date, he could eliminate a number of the keys on the ring. Phillip noted that there were only about fifty left to try in the locks. While he was methodically trying the keys, Mr. Grey told Phillip and Marilee about how the trunks probably came to be in the area. Someone had probably arrived from England with all their worldly possessions in the trunk, and after that, the trunk was probably used only for long trips or to store unused clothing or household goods. Sometimes, they were used as hope chests for young women to keep their quilts and handiwork in until they married.

Suddenly, the key made a clicking noise, and the lock on the largest trunk opened. All were quiet and looked at each other in anticipation. Mr. Grey told Marilee that she should have the honor of opening it, but not knowing what she would find, she wasn't sure she wanted to. Finally, Marilee lifted the heavy lid slowly, only to find an empty tray hiding the cavity of the trunk. More suspense. This time, Phillip lifted the tray out to reveal the inside. Inside, there was what looked like fabric from a man's shirt plus infant clothing and tiny knit booties. There were no letters or notes about who had worn these things or why they had been saved. While Phillip and Marilee discussed the contents, Mr. Grey began working on the second trunk. He tried the last key on the ring but to no avail. None of these keys would work. He did have a solution though and took from his case a package of soft wax. He made an impression of the key hole as best he could, and after writing down the name of the maker of the first trunk, he told Marilee and Phillip that he would go back to his shop and see what he could find. There were hinges on the outside of this trunk, and if need be, he could take it apart to open it, but he would first try all other options.

It was a bit disappointing not only to find nothing revealing in the trunk, but also to be unable to open the second trunk. Marilee had hoped for a story about former residents or at least some significant artifacts. Now, she would have to wait until Mr. Grey could come up with a solution and contact her. She hoped it would happen before Christmas.

She took the contents from the trunk and decided to ask someone at the museum if they could identify the time period of the children's clothing. This would give her something to do while waiting. Marilee put the small clothing on the dining room table so she would remember to take it with her to the museum later in the week. It was difficult to keep on track for the rest of the day as every time she passed the dining room, her thoughts returned to the clothing and the unopened trunk upstairs. That evening, Marilee realized she had completed only one load of laundry the entire day. She would have to go to the museum tomorrow to see about the clothes, or she would never complete the fall cleaning of the guest rooms.

Before falling asleep that night, Phillip and Marilee speculated as to why those specific pieces of clothing had been saved in the trunk. They were very small and would have only fit a very tiny newborn. The stitching was all hand done, and the work on the front of the dress was beautiful. The fabric was fine cotton, the kind used for special garments. The dress was worn in spots that did not make sense if they had been worn by a baby. The buttons at the back seemed more worn than anywhere else, and the bottom of the dress looked as though it had been caught on something and torn. Babies of this size don't usually wear out their clothes. They both hoped it was not because of a tragedy in the family, but of course, infant mortality was common during the early 1800s. Marilee tried to think of more pleasant thoughts as she drifted off to sleep but could only hear soft crying in the distance.

Sending the Letter

Hannah dressed in her work dress and went down to breakfast with her parents. She had hidden her brother's borrowed clothes in a box in the cupboard, hoping no one would find them until she figured out what to do with them. She still had Peter's letter in her pocket as she dared not leave it anywhere in the room for her mother or younger sister to find. She had to find a hiding place to keep it, but she needed time to search out a place where no one would go. She also wanted to write Peter a note, but first, she had to come up with a plan and then she had to find a farmworker whom she could trust to deliver it to Peter. Today would be busy as she had to help get the food ready for lunch and then be sociable to their guests all afternoon. The morning went fast as she helped the cook in the kitchen prepare lunch. They were having a roast of pork, green beans from the garden, roasted potatoes, buttermilk biscuits, and a raspberry tart for dessert. Luckily, the cook sent her to the garden to pick the beans, and while she was there, she watched some of the other farmworkers going about their chores. She noticed the one worker who had delivered the letter from Peter. He seemed to be working nearer the house at the other end of the kitchen garden. Maybe he could deliver a note. Hannah made sure she picked beans from the one row that led to the end of the garden where he was working. When she got to the end, it was only polite to say hello and then she asked him his name and if he knew Peter. He said his name was Joseph, and he knew Peter's father and thought he knew who Peter was. Hannah decided not to ask him at this time if he could deliver a note for her, but she would certainly keep offering to pick things from the garden if needed.

After filling her basket, she hurried back to the kitchen before anyone came to find her. The rest of the morning was busy, and Hannah was pleased she was allowed to make the raspberry tart as she loved to bake. Soon, it was time to get dressed for lunch, and since the family coming was new to the area, her mother had insisted she wear her best summer dress. There was no pocket in this dress, so Hannah tied one of her work pockets around her waist under the dress and kept the letter with her. Hannah really only wanted to stay in her room and think about how to solve her problem and then write a note to Peter.

At lunch, the topic of conversation was, of course, the rumblings of war and who in the area was siding with whom. The women were talking about flowers and recipes, but Hannah kept her ear tuned to the men in case she heard any word about Peter's family. No names were mentioned, but some time frames were mentioned which only made Hannah want to solve her dilemma sooner. The afternoon was spent sitting on the porch making small talk. The new neighbors were nice enough, but Hannah was struggling to keep awake and concentrate on the conversation. Their son was about a year older than Hannah and kept asking her questions about insignificant things. She tried to be polite but did not really have any interest in getting to know him. Finally they left, and Hannah quickly retreated to her room.

She lay on her bed just to think a bit for what seemed like only a few minutes but was awakened to knocking on her door, telling her it was time for supper. After staying out all night, she had fallen asleep and was no closer to a solution about how to be with Peter.

* * *

The next morning, Marilee awoke and quickly worked through the essentials of getting dressed, eating breakfast, and cleaning up so she could go to the museum with the dress she had found in the trunk. Once there, Marilee had to wait until two school groups finished their program with the interpreter. Listening to the discussion about love affairs across the river during war time was quite interesting not only for the students but also for Marilee. She hadn't thought about young relationships being torn apart because families felt the need to choose sides during this conflict. Even though the river was relatively narrow, the current was strong enough to be a deterrent to crossing, just to see a loved one. It made her want to find some books about families separated by the conflict.

Finally, the students moved on to the next part of the program, and Marilee had a chance to talk to Donna, one of the interpreters, and show her the baby dress. Donna had become an interpreter a few years ago because she loved making the history of the area come alive for students. The history, especially the war of 1812, was quite exciting and had really defined the makeup of what this country had become. Marilee asked her where she found information about love affairs that had been ended because of war, and Donna showed her a book someone had written about the families who had been in the area and how their lives had been changed during that period. Marilee decided this would be good spare-time reading material, so she borrowed it to take home. She then removed the dress from her bag and began to tell Donna the story of the trunk in the attic and the dress that was found. Donna carefully examined the dress and agreed with Marilee that it was small and not really the correct proportions for a baby. She thought it looked more like a doll's dress. That might explain the wear around the buttons and hem, but most children did not have toys of this quality. Only the wealthy would have been able to afford toys for their children that included handmade dresses for a doll. This made the story even more mysterious as why was the clothing in the trunk and not the doll? Marilee began to wonder if the doll was in the other trunk and what else might they find there. Donna also became interested and asked to be part of the group when the second trunk was opened. She also knew someone who had lots of keys and would be willing to help them. Marilee had not heard back from Mr. Grey, so together, they set a date for the following Wednesday to try and open the trunk. Marilee suggested they all come for dinner that evening before the grand opening in the attic. Now, she just had to concentrate on getting some Christmas preparations done and try not to think of what was in the trunk.

The next few days were busy. Even though Marilee had thought she was organized for the move, she discovered her Christmas decorations were in several containers and not labeled correctly. Obviously, last Christmas had been put away in a hurry with no thoughts of the move ahead. She did have time to get them organized though as she did not like to put up any decorations until after the American Thanksgiving, which was at the end of the week.

Wednesday came, and Marilee prepared an easy supper because she knew the main event was really trying to open the trunk. Phillip had been somewhat cool about the whole deal as he knew that if nothing was in it, Marilee would be very disappointed. He even said he would clean up after dinner while the rest of the group went up. The group had expanded to include Donna's husband, who was the curator from the museum, and their neighbors, Jeannie and Ralph. Dinner conversation was quite lively, and even though there was anticipation in the air, there did not seem to be a rush to leave the table. Finally, the topic of the trunk came up, and they all, including Phillip, followed Marilee to the attic.

Donna's friend had lent her his keys as he was unable to come that evening, so she began systematically to try the keys in the lock. The third key she tried clicked loudly, and the lock fell open. No one in the room seemed to be breathing as Marilee slowly lifted the lid. The trunk was filled first with homemade quilts and the linens that would have been used for dining. Dinner napkins, which had once been snowy white, were now yellow with age, and on the corner was embroidered a large "E." They all wanted to run to the museum to get a list of some of the family names to see if any started with an "E." There were several table cloths and, farther down, some clothing that had belonged to a young girl. At the bottom were a boys shirt and pants and a hat that was quite worn and had probably belonged to a young boy about fourteen. The mood in the room was decidedly glum as the bottom of the trunk was now visible. As Marilee picked up the pair of pants, she felt a lump of something inside them. Her heart began to race, and she only hoped that it was not a squirrel that had crawled in to die many years ago. There was no smell other than dust, so she carefully took the pants out and opened them up to see what was inside. The first thing she saw was the face and then realized it was that of a doll. Everyone breathed a sigh of relief, and the doll was extracted from the pants. The doll had clothes on it, and the hair tucked under a bonnet was well-worn. The head was made of china, and the painted face was worn. The nose had a chip at the end, and there were no eyebrows left. The mouth was partially worn off, and when you moved the bonnet, the hair moved with it. The hair was probably a wig made from someone's real hair and had become loose over time. This doll had been well-loved. The doll had a black velvet ribbon wrapped tightly around the neck, which did not seem to fit the style, but who knew what young girls were dreaming about when they played with their dolls. The dress that was found in the other trunk would definitely fit this doll. The case of the mysterious dress had been solved, but now the question was to whom had these household goods and the doll belonged? A quiet group deep in thought returned to the downstairs, and the evening of speculation continued over wine and whiskey.

The doll was passed around. After everyone examined it, Marilee tried the other dress on the doll. It fit nicely. The child who had belonged to this doll must have been from a wealthy family, or a well-off relative must have given it as a gift. It may have been brought from Europe when some settlers came to the new world. There were no marks or stamps on the doll to indicate where it had been made. The clothes were certainly finely woven and probably made from Egyptian cotton. The lace could have been from France. Had the boy's clothing and the doll with its accessories belonged to a brother and sister?

Marilee decided to take the hat off to see the hair, and as she did, the wig came off with the bonnet. The hair was made in a similar style as were wigs during that time period. It was soft enough to be real human hair as, of course, synthetics were a modern invention. This had been someone's own hair and made into a doll's wig. It was a lovely auburn color, and the ringlets still had spring to them after all these years. This hair must have been naturally curly.

Without the wig, the doll looked quite disturbing as the top of her head was flat with a small hole in it. Marilee looked in the hole and could see something that looked like paper. Maybe it was the stuffing.

She decided not to pursue the insides tonight for several reasons. First, it was getting late, and second, she wanted to make any discoveries on her own at this point. She would gladly share later when she knew more, so she put the wig back on and tied the bonnet tightly on the doll's head. She announced to the group that that was about as much excitement as she could handle for the evening, and everyone took the hint and made their way to the door. Everyone agreed this had been a fabulous evening, and thanks were said all around for the food, the keys, and the friendships.

After everyone left, Phillip began his promised task of cleaning up the kitchen. He had been as involved as everyone else in the mystery trunk. Marilee helped, and as she did, she told him of her suspicions about the inside of the doll. She would have to figure out a way to get inside without breaking the head or destroying the body. She wasn't even sure if there was anything worthwhile in those cavities. She did know that she was too tired to try and figure it out tonight, so after the dishes had been stacked in the sink to soak, she took the doll and followed Phillip upstairs to bed. Tonight, the doll would sit on a chair in their bedroom, and Marilee hoped she would not dream about the river again.

It was not to be. As she was falling asleep, the mist from the river seemed to be coming into their room, and suddenly, Marilee was enveloped in it.

A Letter to Peter

Hannah had reread Peter's letter so many times that the corners of the paper were beginning to tear. She decided she would have to arrange another meeting at the dock so they could discuss what to do. She took a piece of paper and began to write the note, asking Peter to meet her again in two days. She wanted the note to be only one page, so after the first page was filled, she turned it a quarter turn and continued writing across the first part of the note. This was a way to save paper and postage if a letter had to be mailed. She had seen her mother write letters this way to relatives in England. It took a bit more concentration to read it, but it kept the weight of a letter light. She finished the note by candlelight and then climbed into bed with the note under her pillow. Tomorrow, she hoped she would see Joseph so she could ask him to deliver it.

Morning finally came after what seemed like a very long night. Hannah had finally fallen to sleep, but she kept awakening and always putting her hand under the pillow to check the letter. It was a lovely, sunny day, and Hannah would offer to pick anything needing picking in the garden so she might have the chance to see Joseph.

After breakfast, she volunteered to help the cook in the kitchen. This did not seem unusual as everyone knew Hannah liked to cook and really was a help in the kitchen. She inquired about the garden, and fortunately, there were more beans and peas to be picked, so off she went with a sunbonnet on her head and the precious letter in her pocket.

After about an hour, she noticed Joseph working at the far end of the garden, hoeing weeds. She gradually worked her way to the end, being careful to pick vegetables as she went so as not to attract attention to herself. When she was near Joseph, she stood up, stretched a bit from bending over, and said good morning. Joseph answered, and before anyone could come and interrupt, she asked if he would deliver her letter to Peter. Hesitantly, he agreed and took the letter and put it in his pocket. Now she would just have to wait until the next night and again figure out how to slip out of the house unnoticed at midnight. Hannah worked her way picking vegetables back up the next row and took them in the house to be cooked for lunch. She hoped this would end soon as sending secret messages was very exhausting as was picking vegetables.

The rest of the day was predictable as Hannah helped prepare the vegetables for lunch in a vegetable pie with chicken left from yesterday's dinner. After lunch, Hannah decided she needed to rest, so she went to the attic and sat in the window seat overlooking the river. She could just see the dock poking out from the bushes at the water's edge. Across the river, the trees created a dense growth of leaves, so any movement was obscured. She thought of Peter living on the other side of the river, so close but so far away. The river's current was very fast, and there were several spots where the water swirled in circles. Peter had told Hannah that it was dangerous to travel the river, except in daylight when you could see, and then only if you were an experienced paddler. Peter always stayed close to shore when he came for visits. She wondered if he would ever be able to visit again and that thought saddened her. The effects of working outside most of the morning and eating a hearty lunch soon took a toll on Hannah, and she fell asleep sitting in the window.

When she awoke, Hannah was totally disoriented, and at first, did not know where she was. It had become very hot in the attic, and she needed to get out of there. One last look out the window, though, made her stop and stare. She saw Joseph coming up from the river toward the house. Hannah knew she had to quickly get outside to see if he had a message for her. Quietly but quickly, Hannah went down the three flights of stairs, hoping she would not meet anyone who might ask her to do something or ask her what she was doing in the attic.

When she made it out the front door, she tried to look casual as if nothing was happening. She skipped down the front steps, turned the corner, and ran right into Joseph as he was walking toward the front of the house. He caught her to prevent her from tumbling on the ground. She hoped he had not been going to the house to deliver her message, but she then realized he was carrying a freshly caught fish to take to the cook around the next corner of the house. Feeling disappointed that he had no message for her, she apologized for running into him and was about to continue walking anywhere but here. Joseph then quietly said he had seen Peter on the river and had given him the message. Peter had written his response immediately on top of Hannah's writing to send back to her. Hannah thanked Joseph for his delivery services and continued walking to a shady secluded spot to read her note. It was only a few lines, but it was what she wanted to hear. Peter would meet her at the river at midnight the following evening. Her heart was racing. How would she last until midnight tomorrow?

Just then, she heard her brother calling her as he approached her hiding spot. She quickly shoved the letter in the waistband of her skirt and stepped out into the open. Of course, her brother suspected she was up to something, but Hannah pretended to be hurt by his accusations, so he gave her the message that she was needed in the house. Hannah returned to the kitchen and was asked to help bring some cold food up from the kitchen to the dining room using the dumbwaiter. She was alone for a while downstairs and decided the dumbwaiter might be a good hiding spot for her letter as it kept slipping out of her skirt. She folded up the letter and forced it under the shelf where there was a space between the boards. She would get it later. Now she had to concentrate on the job of getting the food upstairs.

* * *

DECEMBER

December arrived with just a light dusting of snow that made the countryside look like a Christmas card. The snow stuck to the trees but seemed to melt as it touched the pavement. This seemed very civilized as it made it easy to drive but gave you a feeling of anticipation. Marilee looked out into the yard that morning and felt very happy. She loved the Christmas season with carols playing in the stores, parties with friends, decorating with bright shiny colors, and shopping for special gifts. She did feel a bit panicked, though, as she was not as organized this year as she had been in the past. After breakfast, she poured herself another cup of coffee and suggested to Phillip that they sit down together and coordinate some dates for upcoming events. There were several concerts that sounded interesting, and she would have to purchase tickets in advance. Marilee also wanted to have a small party for new friends who had been so kind to them while they were settling into their new lifestyle. Of course, there were also some B&B guests coming to stay, and the bookings had already been made. Phillip had made sure to close off dates when the family would be visiting so no one could book into the B&B. The big weekend was the upcoming weekend when a local group sponsored a house tour of homes that were decorated for the holiday season. Guests were coming on Thursday, and the B&B would be full until Monday morning. It would be a busy weekend. It had been about a month since guests had been at the B&B, and although it had been a nice break, both Phillip and Marilee were looking forward to meeting new guests.

Marilee picked a date for their party, wrote all the important dates on the calendar, and decided that today would be spent decorating the house for the season. The boxes with all the Christmas things were in the basement, and she knew it would take longer to decorate Loyalist House as it was quite different from their previous home. All the decorations would have to find a new place this year. Marilee suggested to Phillip that they check to see if the dumbwaiter in the kitchen would still work as it would be so much easier than carting ten boxes upstairs. Phillip wasn't as excited about that prospect as Marilee but said he would look at it.

Phillip went over to the door that opened to the dumbwaiter, unlocked it, and looked inside. The cables looked OK, so using the handles on the pulley, he began to lower the platform to the basement. Down was easy, but lifting the platform up with weight on it might be a whole new game. Motorizing this might be a good winter project.

Off they went to the basement to find the boxes of decorations. Phillip decided to put one of the smaller boxes on the platform first to see if the cables were strong enough to pull it up one floor. As he started to pull, everything seemed fine, and all was going well until about half way up to the kitchen. Suddenly, one of the cables snapped, and the platform slipped. The box came plunging to the basement, and as Phillip had let go of the pulley, the whole platform came crashing down. There was a lot of noise and dust coming from the shaft of the dumbwaiter. Fortunately, this box of decorations was a plastic container with a tight seal, so nothing had fallen out, and inside the box, things were well-wrapped. The only damage was on the inside of the dumb-waiter. While surveying the damage, Phillip noticed several papers lying at the side of the shaft amongst the broken cables. Thinking they were from the box of decorations, he retrieved them and handed them to Marilee. She gasped as she looked at them. These were not from the box but were letters that had been hidden in the shaft. The paper was yellowed with age, and the handwriting was not done in this century. Someone had deliberately hidden these a long time ago. Marilee decided that today might not be a decorating day after all. She went upstairs, poured herself another cup of coffee, and sat down to look at the letters.

The writing was done in a juvenile fashion but seemed to be two separate sets of handwriting, one much neater than the other. The writing had been done in two different directions on the paper, making it difficult to read. Also, the paper was very brittle, so Marilee had to be careful not to let it crumble. She decided to put it in a plastic sleeve to protect it while she studied it.

Dear Peter,

I must meet you so we can talk about what is going to happen to us. Meet me at the same place and time as the last time we met. I will be listening for your signal.

Love, Hannah

Dear Hannah,

I will be there.

Take Care. Peter

Now Marilee had some names to help her solve the mystery. It was not much to go on, but possibly, the records of families who had lived in the area might reveal a clue such as a family name. Marilee changed into something less dusty and drove into town to the museum to check records. The drive along the river was beautiful today, and a clear view of the other side could be seen as many trees had shed their leaves. There were large homes along the other side of the river just as on this side. Marilee wondered if any had stories to tell similar to theirs. Many people were leery of homes that seemed to have supernatural residents, but Marilee found the possibility to be exciting.

She arrived at the museum and went right to the archives where land deeds were kept. She studied the names of owners of property along the area of the river where their home was but could only find the names of the actual landowner. Of course, only men had owned land,

and women and children were not listed on any records other than as spouse and children. How disappointing! She did, however, find the family names of three families who had lived in close proximity to their property. She quickly copied them down and decided to look up those families through another way. Often, churches kept records of marriages and baptisms, and that might reveal something.

The museum had some old records from churches but not many as the churches in town had been burned. Some several times, so many records had been lost. There had to be another way. She decided that this might not be the time to look as there were more pressing jobs that had to be completed in just a few days. Marilee packed up her notes and drove back along the river to their home, not looking forward to carrying all those boxes up the stairs.

When she arrived at the house, she discovered all the boxes sitting in the front hall. What a nice thing for Phillip to do! Now, Marilee was feeling more like decorating the house for Christmas. The next two days were busy finding new spots for all the snowmen and angels and making sure the matching Christmas balls were evenly spaced on the tree. This year, each of the bedrooms would be decorated as well, so Marilee was thinking a shopping trip might be needed to add to her collection of ornaments. Late that afternoon, Phillip said he was going to the garden center to purchase fresh greens for the outside of the house, so Marilee decided to go as well to see what was new this year in the decorating world.

Once there, Marilee became inspired to rethink the decorating in the bedrooms and not use the old decorations from the past. Phillip found all the greens he needed for the outside, and they returned home, ready to work well into the night. They were totally exhausted from their shopping trip and decided instead to have a nice dinner and decorate tomorrow. During dinner, talk turned to the letter found and what they would do with it. Neither of them knew where to turn next to find out the answers, but suddenly, Marilee remembered that inside the doll there had been some paper. Could they possibly be more letters?

The doll was still sitting in a chair in their bedroom, and Marilee picked it up and took it downstairs. She removed the wig again and looked inside the hole in the head. Marilee tried to hook the paper with a pair of tweezers and twist it so it would be small enough to come through the hole. Unfortunately, that plan did not work. There didn't seem to be any choice but to cut into the body. Marilee still could not let herself do that, so once again, she set the doll aside until she came up with another plan. Now, it was late, so after cleaning up the dinner dishes, Marilee and Phillip went up to bed. Tonight, there would be no dreaming as both Marilee and Phillip were exhausted and fell asleep immediately.

They awoke the next morning to see just a light snow flurry drifting down onto the trees and grass. It really was beginning to look a lot like Christmas. After breakfast, Phillip went outside to work at wrapping the greens around the porch railing and the lamp posts. Marilee went up to the bedrooms to begin decorating each room in a tasteful but practical manner. Since there would be guests staying in the rooms, she wanted it to look festive but not crowded. She decided to do each room in a different Christmas song theme. The large room would be "Angels We Have Heard on High" and have miniature sheet music and instruments on a small tree, with angels scattered around the room. The next room was "O Little Town of Bethlehem," and here, she used her nativity scene on a table as the centre piece. She had a collection of sheep which were used in various spots as well. The room where the grandchildren would sleep at Christmas was "Santa Claus is Coming to Town," and there were a variety of Santas sitting everywhere. The fourth room would represent "I Saw Three Ships," and Phillip's collection of sail boats would be used as decorations to compliment the nautical theme in the room. The last room would be "We Three Kings," and gold and purple were the dominant colors, with statues of kings and camels located on the tables. Marilee was quite proud of her decorating and went downstairs to see how Phillip was doing. He had completed the outside and was busy trying to repair the broken dumbwaiter. They decided it was not fixable without major repairs, so they locked the doors to the shaft and put the key in a safe place.

The next few days flew by as there was shopping to do and baking for the weekend guests. Finally, on Thursday at noon, the beds were made, most of the food preparation done, and Loyalist House was once again ready to receive guests. It certainly looked festive both outside and in, with just the right amount of snow on the ground. Two couples arrived precisely at four that afternoon. They seemed nice but somewhat distant and a bit demanding. They asked if they could have breakfast in their room as they liked to be alone in the morning. Marilee explained that the rooms were not set up for this, and most people really did enjoy eating together in the dining room. They conceded, but one couple wanted breakfast at seven, and the other couple at eight-thirty. This was not going to be the easy weekend Marilee had envisioned. She would have to serve something in individual serving dishes so they could be cooked at different times.

The next couple arrived about an hour later and were very friendly and so pleased to be there for the weekend. They were willing to eat at whatever time was convenient, so Marilee suggested breakfast at eight-thirty. Marilee had assigned them to the "I Saw Three Ships" room, and they were delighted to see the nautical theme as they both loved to sail. She hoped the other couples would be as happy with their rooms as well. She figured if there were no complaints, that would be a positive response. As soon as the couples were settled in, Marilee quickly went to the kitchen to see if she had all the ingredients for ham and egg cups as these could be made individually and as needed. She had purchased asparagus for a frittata, but she could steam it instead and serve it beside the egg cups. She now needed to ask if anyone disliked any foods so she could alter recipes. Marilee was very good at substituting ingredients when guests had dislikes or allergies, perceived or real. It did annoy her, though, when someone said they were allergic to eggs and then were observed eating muffins without asking about ingredients. Marilee called this a "visible-egg allergy." Of course, the guests were always correct. Later in the evening, she was able to find out what everyone could or could not eat for breakfast. The early risers only wanted toast and tea at seven, while the eight-thirty group was happy with the planned breakfast.

The next morning, at exactly seven, the early risers sat down at the dining room table. Not a word was spoken, only a polite thank-you for the breakfast. Phillip offered them the morning newspaper and again, just a polite thank-you. These were definitely not morning people. They continued to sit and read the paper and drink tea until well after eight. The other two couples appeared shortly before eight-thirty and began talking. It was always surprising how much strangers had in common when they got to know each other. Breakfast service began, and the first couple put aside the paper and joined in the conversation. As Marilee was serving the ham and egg cups, the early risers declared that they were ready for their breakfast now as well and would also like the main entree. This could have been a disaster as the entree took at least twenty-five minutes to cook, but Marilee had made extras in case anyone wanted seconds. Leftovers always made a welcome lunch for her and Phillip as well. She hoped she did not show the surprise on her face while in the dining room, but once back in the kitchen, Phillip knew something had annoyed her just by her expression. Quietly, she told Phillip the request, and he too was nonplussed at the nerve of some people. It got them thinking it might be a good idea to make a space upstairs where guests could make their own morning tea or coffee and toast before breakfast. People were such creatures of habit that even when away they needed the same routine, no matter the inconvenience to others. Breakfast proceeded nicely after that, and everyone joined in the conversation. They all had tickets for the house tour, so no one really lingered too long after nine-thirty. This was great as Marilee was meeting Jeannie to tour the houses as well. Phillip said he would clean up in the kitchen and vacuum as soon as the guests left. Marilee quickly went up to refresh the bathrooms and remake beds. As these guests had booked a two night stay, it was an easy task.

Each December, a local service club presented a tour of several professionally decorated homes in the area. Some were historic homes, while others were more modern, but all had interesting architectural features and gave visitors great ideas for seasonal decorating. The money raised was given to local charities and was always well-attended, regardless of the weather. Marilee and Jeannie decided to start about noon as they figured the morning crowd would be stopping for lunch about then. They could always finish any unseen houses the next day as it was a two-day event. They were not disappointed as several of the large mansions built in the late 1800s were on the tour this year. Wealthy American industrialists had built these homes as summer places, and now, they were restored and used as B&B's or weekend homes. It was a chance to use your imagination and see how the wealthy might have lived.

There was also a very small cottage on the tour this year, and even though it was a quarter of the size of the mansions, it was very cozy and well-proportioned. It was always interesting to learn about the history of the home, and this particular house had a door hidden in the woodwork, which led to a secret tunnel and to buildings that had been in the back yard. One could imagine all kinds of activities that may have entered through that door, from illegal goods to slaves being hidden on their way to freedom.

Marilee and Jeannie managed to see all the houses in one afternoon as they seemed to be in-between the serious early morning group and the latecomers who had probably stopped for a leisurely lunch and were enjoying their day. They ended up at a very ultramodern home, decorated in shades of pink and lime-green. It did not actually evoke a Christmas spirit in the viewers, but it certainly stimulated conversation as people went through the house. As unusual as the colors were, they seemed right for the style of the home. It wasn't everyone's taste, but that was the purpose of selecting different homes and decorators. Marilee and Jeannie returned to Loyalist House and enjoyed a glass of wine while rehashing all the decorating ideas. When Phillip returned from volunteering as a guide at the museum, he also had interesting tales to tell about the visitors who had come to the museum and the many questions that they had asked. The museum was also on the tour, and the current display of artifacts always brought a number of interesting people, mostly husbands not wanting to go through the houses.

Shortly, their guests returned from the tour, and of course, the conversation turned to what was now called the "pink and green" house. Phillip offered everyone a glass of wine, the conversation continued, and even though they had all seen the same homes, each had a different point of view and opinion. It seemed as though all the couples had relaxed, especially the early risers who were now very talkative. Marilee and Phillip had noticed that when some of their guests arrived, they were quite tense and still in work mode, but after a good night's sleep and time spent in town, their easygoing vacation side appeared.

Everyone had plans for dinner, so the group went to their rooms to freshen up before leaving for the restaurant. Marilee, Phillip, and Jeannie called Jeannie's husband and asked him to come over for supper. They decided to order Chinese food, and when Ralph arrived, the men drove to pick up dinner. They spent the evening enjoying the dinner and planning the Christmas party Marilee was having the next weekend. She had sent out invitations, and Jeannie insisted that she let her help with the food preparation. By the end of the evening, they had only to shop and cook and enjoy themselves next week. The guest list included five couples who were all neighbors. Some had just moved here in the past few years, and others were longtime residents.

The next morning, the early risers repeated their morning ritual of tea and toast at seven, read the newspaper, and then had breakfast with the rest of the group at eight-thirty. Marilee was prepared today and had made a large batch of baked apple French toast, so there was enough food for all. She would be ready tomorrow morning as well and would make her triple cheese strata, which served ten. Tonight was a concert at one of the churches in town, so if she did all her prepping for Sunday breakfast before tonight, it would be easier than after coming in late from the concert. That was the great thing about some of these recipes. They could be almost completely made the night before and refrigerated overnight. The next morning, just pop it in the oven, and the main entree was ready. Marilee thought she should write a B&B cookbook of all her favorite recipes, but that would have to wait until much later.

Sunday morning arrived, everyone was delighted with breakfast, and by ten-thirty, all the guests had left Loyalist House. Now, the cleanup could begin. There was no real hurry as there were no more paying guests until April, only family for Christmas and some friends in February. The house did need to be cleaned for the party next weekend, but that was six days away.

Once again, the week flew by with preparations for the party and Christmas shopping for the family. Tonight was the party, and the food was ready. The house was sparkling with lights and decorations. Marilee and Phillip were dressed in their finest and anxiously awaiting the arrival of their guests. The first to arrive were Jeannie and Ralph as they were bringing some of the goodies. Jeannie was a fabulous baker, so she had made several appetizers that were pastry with different fillings inside. She had also made an assortment of Christmas cookies and cakes for dessert. Marilee had made classic vegetable crudités and several dips. There was a spinach salad with pears and pecans, roasted chicken with sour cherry sauce sweetened with maple syrup, grilled asparagus, and quinoa with lemon zest. No one would go home hungry tonight.

The other guests all seemed to be on the same time schedule and arrived together. After introductions, they all sat in the living room and politely exchanged news of who was ready for Christmas, where they were spending the holidays, how nice the weather was, and would it last. It all seemed a bit stilted. Marilee hoped the evening would not remain this way. Phillip served drinks, passed the appetizers, and gave Marilee a concerned look. Jeannie was watching and suddenly changed the conversation to the doll Marilee had found in the trunk in the attic. It became very quiet, and everyone was watching Marilee to see what she would say. Sensing that she had no other option, she decided to tell the group the story so far.

She relayed the story of the trunks, finding a key to open them, finding clothes first, and then the doll. She included the story of the letter in the dumbwaiter but decided not to go as far as her dreams of hearing crying noises and footsteps in the attic. She didn't want to scare anyone. To her surprise, her neighbor up the road, who also lived in an historic home, began to tell a similar story. Anne and Joe's home was closer to town and had been rebuilt after the town had been burned in 1813. It had belonged to a family who were instrumental in the settlement of the area. It had been sold several times over the years, and additions had been made and taken off and added again, so it did not have the architecture of just one period.

Anne began to tell the story of hearing noises in the upper part of the original structure and one of the additions. She said that at night they would not only hear footsteps, but also mumbling. It sounded as though people were trying to talk quietly about something. It went on for about six years after they had moved in until they decided they had to find a way to make it stop or move. They had decided to renovate and remove one of the more recent additions and replace it with something that complimented the style of the original house. Even though the noises had bothered Anne, she had felt that if the part of the house where the spirits resided was removed, there might be angry spirits instead of just noisy spirits. After researching the topic on the internet, Anne had found a person who would rid the house of spirits and release them so they could continue on their path. Apparently, some spirits became trapped in a place after their death because of circumstances that left them unhappy or distraught with those left behind. It had all seemed plausible, and if it worked, Anne and Joe would not have to share their home with an unhappy spirit.

The date had been set for this modern ghostbuster to come to their home and release the spirit. When he had arrived, he had looked a bit odd with a very long beard and clothes that were several decades old. Joe had thought that maybe he was a spirit himself. He had introduced himself as Manfred and entered their home, mostly looking up at the ceiling. He had asked a lot of questions about the age of the home, noises they had heard, incidents that had happened that might be attributed to paranormal behavior and if there had been any violent actions. He had then toured the house alone, including the attics. When he had returned downstairs, he had sat with Anne and Joe and told them they had more than one spirit, in fact, he had felt there were five sprits in the house. He had said some had died in the home; some were young and some old. One female spirit had tragically lost her fiancé in a farm accident weeks before the wedding. Anne and Joe had wondered how he could find out all this information in an hour, but had been willing to listen to how to fix the situation. He had said he would perform a ritual similar to a funeral that would release all the spirits to the next world and then Joe and Anne could begin their renovation. A date had been set for the ritual, and they had both felt a bit guilty about trying to get these spirits out of this house but also relieved that the spirits could move on and not be stuck in a spot where they were unhappy.

Manfred had returned the next week, and together, they had performed the ritual release. He had statements for them to read, and he seemed to do a lot of chanting, but after forty-five minutes, it had ended. They had chatted a bit about his job and the places it took him, but Manfred really was not the kind of guy to chat idly. Joe had paid Manfred, and Manfred had promised if any of the paranormal behavior returned, they should call him, and he would be back as he guaranteed his work. That night, Anne and Joe had not been able to get to sleep as they were waiting for some noises to begin. Nothing had happened, and after a month of no noise, they had begun their renovations. To this day, they had not heard any strange sounds in the attic of the old part or the new part of the house.

The group could not quite believe this story and were waiting for Anne and Joe to say it had all be a joke, but that didn't happen. Everyone asked questions about the story until Marilee announced that dinner was ready in the dining room. After hearing this story, Marilee wasn't sure if she wanted to get rid of the spirit upstairs. She thought it would be better to wait until she found out more information about the doll and the letters.

Over dinner, the conversation remained on the topic of ghosts. With the area being so old and having witnessed so much conflict, it would not be a surprise if every home had a resident spirit.

All during dinner, one couple, Mary and Bill, listened but rarely spoke. Bill looked at Mary at one point and asked if he should tell the story or would she. Mary said he could tell it. They lived in a home in the town that was built in the 1980s as the original house had been a small postwar house that needed a lot of work to make it livable. They had torn the house down and built a lovely Queen Anne-style home on the property. There was an old barn at the back of the lot that had remained and was still used for storage today. When they had purchased the property through an estate sale, everything in the barn had been left behind and had become theirs. They had discovered an old car that had turned out to be a 1920s vintage. It had not been in good shape but it had been worth restoring. Bill's son had decided to take on the project and had visited on weekends and spent all his time in the barn, fixing this car. After what had seemed like an eternity, Bill and John had finished the car, and it had been ready to drive. It had been an open-style vehicle, so being summer, they had decided to take it for a drive one sunny weekend. Bill and John had sat in front, and Mary and John's wife Joan had sat in the back. It had been a delightful way to see the countryside, and when they had returned home, they had taken photos of everyone in the car, just the driver in the car, and the car parked beside the barn with no one in it. The car had been used for special occasions on sunny days after that, and eventually, John had moved the car to his country property, where the storage situation was more protective and secure. The pictures had been developed and admired and then put in an album and forgotten. One day, Mary had been going through some of the albums, trying to get rid of extra possessions, and she had come across all the photos that had been taken that first day. She could not believe it when the photo she had seen with Bill in the driver's seat also had a stately lady in period dress, sitting very erect in the back seat, looking right at the camera. The image had been slightly hazy, but you could distinguish the clothes and hat she was wearing. If Mary had not been there that day, she would have believed someone had been dressed up for the photo, but she knew that that was not the case. It had really given her shivers as she had continued to look at the other pictures to see if the lady was in any others, but she was not. They had been sitting in that very seat where the image had appeared. Mary had called Bill, and he had been shocked as well. Had the spirit of this woman been in the barn all this time, and was she still there? They had immediately called their son and told him the story, but he hadn't noticed anything unusual while working on the car. The question now had been: had the women stayed with the car, or was her spirit still in their barn? Bill and Mary had tried to find out about the family who had lived in the home before they had rebuilt, but no one had seemed to remember anything about the family. They had decided to try and forget the incident, but of course, they still had the photo. John had taken subsequent photos of the car, but no surprise images appeared. Mary had decided she just wouldn't go to the barn anymore, and Bill, with the help of a friend, had cleared most of the old equipment out, and it now just stored garden equipment. He always made sure he whistled whenever he entered the building.

No one had heard this story before, and so the conversation really became intense with speculation about who it was, and where was she now? They could go to the town offices to find records or go on a property database to see who had owned the house previously, and they all decided they would have to do this. They might have to invite Manfred back to release this poor woman.

Marilee decided to serve dessert in the living room as they had been sitting for a long time, listening to stories. It felt good to get up and move around. The rest of the evening returned to more normal conversations as no one else had a ghost story to tell. When the clock in the hall stuck twelve, everyone decided they had to get home. Marilee called them all "Cinderellas," and "Merry Christmas" was wished all around as they left. Jeannie whispered to Marilee and Phillip as she left that they could never have planned a party like that, no matter how hard they'd tried.

Marilee and Phillip gathered up the dishes, put the food away, and turned on the dishwasher. The rest of the cleanup would wait until tomorrow. Marilee hoped that after all the stories she had heard tonight, she would not dream of mist and crying. She must have been extremely tired as it seemed like ten minutes from the time her head hit the pillow until the phone rang at eight o'clock the next morning.

It was Jeannie on the phone. She had an idea about how they could help Mary and Bill solve their ghost mystery. She would pick Marilee up at nine o'clock on Monday morning, and they would go and research some properties at the town office. She had been unable to sleep most of the night, thinking about this. Marilee was glad she hadn't been up all night and agreed to go with Jeannie on Monday. Right now, Marilee just needed coffee, so she went downstairs, poured her coffee, and started cleaning the kitchen.

Monday morning arrived, and right on time, Jeannie arrived to pick up Marilee. Phillip declined their invitation to join them as he had some paper work to do. They drove to the town office and were directed to a room in the basement where many very large books were kept. The clerk told them they could use any books in the room and described the system used for recording property owners as well as births and deaths. This was beginning to look like a larger task than they had imagined.

Two hours later, they had discovered the three previous owners of Bill and Mary's property and that the last owner's wife had died six months before her husband. Now, they were really curious about how she died. Jeannie went upstairs and asked the clerk if there were any newspaper clippings of local events kept at this office. Again, they were directed to another basement room with an assortment of files, some on microfiche, some digital, and others actually still in newspaper format. Unifying all these files would make a good summer-works project for a student.

They eventually found an article about a woman who had been killed in a crash while riding in an antique car after attending a parade. It had been tragic, and her husband had been devastated and died six months later—of a broken heart, many had said. This had probably been the woman in the picture. Now they knew who she was and why she was still in the car.

Marilee and Jeannie had a copy made of the article and drove immediately to Bill and Mary's. They both decided that Bill and Mary needed to call Manfred to help them release this woman and, possibly, her husband. He could also be haunting the barn.

Bill and Mary didn't seem as excited about it as Jeannie and Marilee were but accepted the copy of the article and showed the photo of the car to them before they left. They really felt they would have to think about this whole release thing. They were pleased Marilee and Jeannie had discovered the story and were anxious to tell their son the next time they saw him.

Marilee and Jeannie found a quiet spot to have a late lunch, rehashed their findings, and wondered if they might be invited to see Manfred release the spirit of the lady in the car. After lunch, they returned home, and as the day was almost over, Marilee decided to wrap some Christmas presents as it was too late to begin anything serious.

The next ten days flew by with Christmas preparations, visiting with friends, and having everything ready when the family arrived Christmas Eve. There had been no time for Marilee to think about noises in the attic or releasing spirits in friends' barns. It had begun to snow that afternoon and really did look like a scene from a Christmas card. Everyone arrived in time for supper that night, and as expected, the children were very excited. After supper, Phillip took the boys to the computer and showed them how technology could track Santa and his sleigh. They saw that he was already delivering toys to girls and boys in Europe. This increased the excitement level considerably but did get the boys wanting to hang their stocking and go to bed. The baby just watched and laughed at the running around, not really caring about Santa this year. Stockings were hung, the story *The Night Before Christmas* was read, but the excitement level was not allowing for an easy bedtime. Finally, after several parental interventions, the boys settled down and went to sleep.

The adults all gathered downstairs to enjoy some Christmas treats while assembling toys and stuffing stockings. It looked like Christmas Day would be full of fun and excitement, playing with new toys. Marilee finished some food preparation in the kitchen so it would be easy to stuff the turkey and have it in the oven to be ready for an early afternoon dinner. She always made brunch dishes that were prepared the night before: baked poached eggs and a coffee cake made from frozen dough balls. It had been their daughters' favorite for many years, and since it was easy, Marilee always included it for Christmas morning. The rest of the evening was spent catching up on news of friends and relatives, and it wasn't long until everyone figured it might be a good idea to get some sleep as small children wake up early, especially on Christmas morning.

Owen woke up with a start. He was sure he heard it. "Ho Ho Ho." He really heard it that time! Santa must be downstairs. Just then, Grandpa and Grandma walked into the room. They had their housecoats and their glasses on and seemed to be ready for morning. Grandpa asked him if he had heard Santa. Owen said he thought Santa was downstairs right now. While they were looking for slippers, Jonathon, who was five-and-a-half, woke up and said as it was light out, so Santa would already be back at the North Pole. Though he thought he may have heard bells once in the night. Owen agreed with his older brother that he had heard them as well. The parents and baby Amanda were up now, and the whole family went downstairs together. Cameras were rolling to get Christmas morning reactions. It was a chaotic scene with squeals of glee as new toys were discovered. Everything seemed to have a siren or a whistle. Amanda just wanted to tear the paper but did like her soft teddy bear. Marilee brought coffee into the living room for the adults, and they watched the children play. It was delightful to see Christmas morning through the eyes of innocent children. Soon, breakfast was ready, and as usual, the food brought back fond memories of past Christmases for the girls. There wasn't to be much lingering at the table, though, as Owen and Jonathon had received new sleds, and since there was snow outside, they wanted to try them out. Everyone got dressed and ready for an outdoor adventure. Marilee said she would go out for a bit but had to work on dinner soon.

Just up the road near the path was a small hill that would be just the right size for sledding, so off they all went to see how the new sled worked. The boys never tired of going down or being pulled around by their dads. The women decided to go back to the house so Amanda could nap, and they could all work on getting dinner ready.

The rest of the day went quickly, the dinner was perfect, the children played nicely, and there was pleasant conversation. It really had been one of the best Christmases yet. Maybe it was because the children were just the right age for excitement, or maybe it was the good vibes the house emitted, but whatever it was, Marilee and Phillip decided as they were falling asleep that they should always celebrate Christmas in this house.

The next thing Marilee heard was someone crying, but this time, it seemed to be in the hall outside her door. She suddenly realized she was not dreaming and that it was one of the children. It seemed that Owen had gone downstairs when he woke up, only to discover that Santa had not come last night. He was distraught. Marilee then had to explain how it was only one night that Santa came, and after that, he was so tired that when he returned to the North Pole, he slept for at least a week. A week was as long a time period that Owen could imagine. He accepted the answer but was still disappointed. A breakfast of oatmeal with bananas and maple syrup did seem to help change his mood.

The families had to pack up and leave as they were both travelling to visit the other grandparents for another Christmas. Marilee and Phillip had been invited to join their daughter Janine and Gary at his parents' home but had declined. They were looking forward to a few quiet days at home. It might get nice enough to go for a walk along the river.

After everyone left, Marilee decided to leave the cleanup until tomorrow and just relax and begin to read one of the new books she had received as a gift. Phillip was good with that idea as well as he wanted to begin a woodworking project now that he had new carving tools.

Phillip had found a newly written history book of the area at the museum and had given it to Marilee for Christmas. It might have some information that would help her discover more about the people who had lived in the nearby homes. She sat in her favorite chair by the window in the family room. From there, she could see the river and across to the houses on other side. This was the perfect spot to read a history book about the area. Suddenly, Phillip came into the room and asked why she was reading in the dark. Marilee looked at him strangely and then realized she had been reading for three hours, and it was beginning to get dark outside. Lights were on in houses across the river, and only the outline of the trees could be seen from her window. This was a good book. Now Marilee just wanted to read and find out more details about the war that had taken place in the area. Practicality overcame her, though, as well as hunger, and she followed Phillip to the kitchen, where they created a small replica of Christmas dinner from the leftovers.

After dinner, they cleaned up the kitchen and decided to read in their room as they really were tired from all the seasonal festivities. This way, if they fell asleep, they would already be in bed. It didn't take long, and by 10:00 p.m., both were sound asleep with the lights on.

Morning came, and routines took over as there was laundry to do and the house needed cleaning. No guests were coming until February, but Marilee did not want to leave the cleanup any longer. They had been invited to a friend's house for a New Year's Eve party, so they would be gone for a few days. It would be nice to come home to a neat house.

In-between all the cleaning, Marilee and Phillip did find time to take several walks along the river. With just the right amount of snow on the ground, the landscape looked like a winter wonderland. The tree branches were white, but you could still see through them and realize the shape of the tree. In summer, you couldn't differentiate between the round maples and the columnar poplars because of the abundant foliage. Today, you could even see the houses across the river. Most were large, multi-storied, white-frame houses. These homes had probably been built in the mid-twentieth century by wealthy industrialists who had spent their summers in the area. The shoreline for these homes was very steep, and there were several elaborate staircases from the home down to the river's edge. You would certainly want to remember everything when going down to spend time on the dock. It seemed that every season changed the scenery along the river, and winter was certainly not disappointing.

The rest of the week went by quickly, and soon, Marilee and Phillip were packing the car to visit their friends. When they returned it, would be a new year.

JANUARY

January began with a raging snow storm with high winds and great amounts of snow. It was unusual for the area to get a lot of snow, and many residents had prided themselves on living in an area that was protected and brought with it bragging rights about mild winters. This Sunday was a different story. If the snow ploughs were out, they had not been along the river road. A phone message had been left that church was cancelled, which apparently never happened. It would be a good day to build a fire in the fireplace and read a book. Marilee and Phillip would have done just that, but they were stranded at their daughter's place. They had stopped there on the way home as the roads had deteriorated quickly on the drive home. It was as good an excuse as any to visit and play with their grandchildren. The weather gurus were saying the storm would be over by midnight, so they could return home tomorrow. For now, the order of the day was relaxing, playing, napping, and eating.

The children had received new board games for Christmas, and each one had to be tried out. After two hours of games aimed at preschoolers, lunch was a welcomed event. After lunch, new stories were read, and it was nap time for the youngest and quiet time for his brother. The adults enjoyed visit over a quiet cup of tea. Phillip and Marilee were planning a trip south this winter and were telling Janine and Gary about their plans. They wanted to rent a home for several weeks somewhere south, where it was warm, but they hadn't really looked into it yet. It was still snowing like crazy outside, and the more they thought about it, the idea just seemed to get better. The afternoon and evening continued in a relaxed fashion, and fortunately, the snowfall tapered off after dinner. An extra day spent with family really was a bonus after a busy holiday season.

The next morning dawned clear and crisp, with the main roads reporting they had been ploughed, so Phillip and Marilee packed up after breakfast and headed home, not sure how much snow would be in their driveway. The drive was easy, and the traffic was light, but there was quite a bit of snow piled at the side of the roads. The closer they came to their road, the higher the snow banks were at each driveway. This really had been a significant snowfall. When they reached their driveway, they were pleasantly surprised to see the driveway ploughed all the way back to the carriage house. The sidewalk was shoveled to the front door and to the back. Since Phillip had not contracted anyone to clean the driveway this winter, he was surprised to see this. When he got to the back door, there was a note stuck in the handle. Their neighbor, Ralph, had sent the guy who ploughed his driveway over to do Phillip's because he knew they were away. Phillip decided to call the company and arrange for him to continue ploughing, especially if this type of winter was a trend.

The rest of the day was spent unpacking and doing laundry. By late afternoon, Phillip had built a fire in the fireplace, and they both spent a lovely evening enjoying a TV supper and a movie in the cozy living room. It had been a busy few days at the end of a wonderful holiday. Bed and restful sleep would certainly be welcomed tonight. But it was not to be, for just as Marilee was drifting off, she heard the familiar whistling noises on the river.

The Proposal

Hannah was sitting behind the bushes by the river bank, waiting for Peter. She had managed to get out of the house without any one seeing her, but it had been close. The cook had just been finishing some preparation for the next day in the kitchen and had just stepped back into the kitchen from the hall as Hannah had been about to walk by. She had quickly hidden behind a server in the hall and was pretty sure she hadn't been seen. The waiting part of these rendezvous was always the worst part as Hannah always worried that Peter might be seen and would have to turn back before they met. Suddenly, Hannah stepped out of the bushes just as Peter reached the dock. In the dark silent night, they embraced, glad that the meeting was finally here. They returned behind the bushes and started to talk about how their friendship could continue despite the war.

"Where do you keep all the letters we are exchanging?" asked Peter.

Hannah told him she kept them in her pocket or under her pillow at night for now, but she had been looking for a hiding place where no one would look. She had thought about a trunk in the attic, but it could be borrowed at any time by someone who needed it, so that didn't seem like a good place. She told Peter she would continue to look the next day for a safe place to keep the letters, where only she might think to look.

"How are we going to see each other if your family moves across the river?" asked Hannah.

Peter began to tell her about his trip with his father to the other side of the river to find a new home. He said the whole family would be leaving in two days, taking as much of the livestock and household goods they could manage to put into one cart. He also told her that the property they had secured had no house, but there was enough land to set up a farm and build a house. They would be living in makeshift buildings until something was built. His father hoped to have something completed before winter. Peter also told about how they had surveyed the land right up to the river while they were there, and he thought he could see their old property and Hannah's parents' property across the river. If this was true, he figured they could continue to meet in secret, and when this disagreement was over, they could marry. Peter hadn't asked Hannah to marry him, but now, he took both her hands and asked if she would marry him after the disagreement between the two countries was settled. Hannah, of course, said yes and asked Peter how long he thought that might be. Of course, he didn't know the answer to that but hoped it would be maybe a year. Peter suddenly moved very close to Hannah, and for the first time, he kissed her. Hannah's heart skipped a beat, and a warm feeling enveloped her, and for just a moment, all the perils and difficulties they encountered disappeared. Then she was suddenly aware again of the old dirty clothes belonging to her brother that she was wearing.

She wished this wonderful moment had taken place under better circumstances and realized she would not be able to tell anyone about the good news.

Peter then continued to tell her how he thought they could meet at the river. It would be more difficult as there would be no way to get letters to each other, and they would need to be careful as now he would be considered an enemy on this side of the river. He thought that for the rest of the summer and part of the fall, they could try to meet on the fifth day of the month, at midnight by the dock. If the weather was bad, they would have to wait until the next month, and they would only wait half an hour for the other person to show up. Peter then gave Hannah a letter and told her to read it after she was safely in the house. It was then time for him to return home. One last kiss and a long embrace, and they separated. Peter rowed back up the river along the shore while Hannah watched, tears streaming down her face.

* * *

January turned out to be a harsh month weather wise. It seemed to Marilee that there was a snowstorm every week. This was somewhat unsettling as this area was supposed to be milder than most in the province. For several nights, the windmills had kept the grapevines from freezing, and this sounded as though helicopters were flying over the house most of the night.

Many of their neighbors started leaving for southern parts, and Marilee and Phillip decided to look for a place in the sun for a month as well. Florida seemed like a good place to start, and after several days on the internet and a lot of e-mails, they found a place near the beach and far enough south to guarantee at least warm temperatures if not hot. They would have a place to stay for three weeks in February, and they hoped that by then the weather here would start to temper. Because February was often when people started contacting Loyalist House for reservations, Phillip figured out how they could still receive all their calls and internet contacts while away.

There were a few chores to be done around the house before they left, and by the end of January, Marilee and Phillip were ready to fly to Florida for a warm vacation. Marilee was disappointed she had not found time to explore the inside of the doll to see what was in there, but that could wait until March. Before they left, she had made a list of all the things she might look for while in Florida that would be useful at the B&B.

Their departure date came, the flights were on time, and by the end of the day, they were sitting by a pool, sipping wine, enjoying a warm, sunny day. *This could be habit-forming,* thought Phillip. Maybe they would plan to do this every year and maybe for longer than three weeks. But a small voice in his head kept asking questions: would he get bored? Would he get tired of joining Marilee on her shopping ventures? How many books could he read? Would they miss their family too much? He would just have to wait to find out the answers, but for now, he would try and enjoy this welcomed change in lifestyle.

FEBRUARY

Every day seemed to dawn sunny and warm, with birds singing and palm trees blowing in the breeze. People went about their business as though this weather was the norm. Often, if a late-afternoon shower would pop up, anyone caught outside seemed offended that it would rain in this perfect climate. Marilee and Phillip certainly enjoyed the warmth, but somehow, it just didn't feel right. Maybe it was guilt, thinking about all the friends and relatives left behind to endure the snow, slush, and cold. They did try to get involved in some of the activities in their community, but most of them revolved around dancing, golf, or playing cards. Also, there was always drinking involved at every event, and Phillip thought if he stayed here long, he could own a winery with the money he would be spending, buying wine. Marilee didn't really like golf or dance, and she was a really bad cardplayer, so she spent much of her time either walking on the beach or visiting the shopping areas for bargains. She figured she was spending as much money putting in time as it would cost to take a fabulous cruise.

They were both glad they had tried this new lifestyle out before choosing any permanent winter adventure.

By the third week, both Marilee and Phillip were ready to return home to Loyalist House. Marilee began thinking about all the things she wanted to do in the house when she returned and, in particular, to investigate the inside of the doll to see what was there. She had done some research on the internet and had read a number of stories about slaves leaving the south to travel to safety in the north via the underground railway. There were several stories of not only items, but also actual people being hidden in strange, small places so as not to be discovered. She wondered if this practice had been around earlier than the Civil War era.

There were a lot of history stories to keep her interested, but none ever mentioned about the wailing noises she often thought she heard in their attic. Ghost stories she investigated did tell about noises and crying if a house was haunted, but Marilee really didn't want to think she lived in a haunted house.

She and Phillip did discuss what they would do if they discovered the house might be haunted. If they sold it, they would have to disclose that information to a prospective buyer, but no one had told them when they had bought. Guests might not want to stay in a haunted B&B, and that would be the end of their current venture. The value of their property might go down as it might not be as saleable if it was known as being haunted. On the other hand, it could be a selling feature to some people. Phillip suggested that if that was the case, they could contact a TV producer and make a reality show about running a haunted B&B.

They both decided they had way too much time on their hands, sitting in the sunshine, and really did need to get back to being more productive.

Three days later, they were flying home, and even when below freezing temperatures greeted them as they walked to the car, they were still happy to be home.

Maybe a twelve-day cruise to a warm climate would be a better idea as a winter break next year.

When they arrived at Loyalist House, everything looked just as they had left it. Phillip turned up the furnace and built a fire in two of the fireplaces to take the chill from the house. After a light supper and a glass of good local wine, they were both ready for bed by early evening. Both Phillip and Marilee slept soundly and awoke to a bright, sunny morning, but the trees outside their window looked like sticks rather than palm trees. They suddenly remembered they were home, and it was still winter here.

Marilee decided that now that she was home, she would be a bit selfish with her time for a few days and spend it investigating what was inside the doll. After breakfast, she quickly popped in a load of laundry and went to the bedroom to retrieve the doll. She had left it sitting on the chair in their bedroom after the dinner party, but when she entered the bedroom, the first thing her eyes saw was an empty chair with no doll. She panicked slightly but then figured she had placed it somewhere else before they had gone to Florida. She searched their bedroom, followed by the guest rooms, the laundry room, and the sitting room. Still no doll. Now she was beginning to panic. Either she was really bad at remembering, or someone had broken into the house while they were away and had stolen the doll. She went down to the main floor, found Phillip, and told him about her discovery. He looked concerned but said he had not noticed anything disturbed or missing and no sign of forced entry, but he would check the basement windows to be sure. Marilee searched every room and every cupboard on the main floor but did not find the doll. Phillip returned from the basement with no answers to the problem. They now did not know whether to call the police or just keep looking. This was all very disheartening as Marilee had felt she was getting close to solving the mystery, and opening up the doll might have been the answer. Now, she had gone back several steps in the plan. They decided to systematically search each room together, hoping they had missed a spot. After an hour, they knew where all their possessions were in the house but not the doll.

The rest of the day was spent looking again in cupboards and closets or talking about where it might be. Neither Phillip nor Marilee accomplished any work, and by dinner time, Marilee remembered the laundry was still in the washing machine, waiting to be put in the dryer. Over dinner, when they tried to think of the next step, they realized they had not checked the attic. Marilee knew she had not taken the doll up there, but then again, maybe she had and had forgotten about it. Leaving their half-finished dinner on the table, they quickly went up the back stairs and on up to the attic. Unfortunately, they were disappointed as no doll was anywhere to be seen either on or under the few pieces of furniture in the attic.

The rest of the evening was very quiet as both Phillip and Marilee were lost in their own thoughts about the missing doll. Marilee was thinking that if they hadn't gone to Florida, this might never have happened. Phillip was thinking this whole history business might be getting out of hand as it was beginning to consume their lives. Neither slept well that night as they still wondered if someone had broken into their home while they were away, and this thought really felt like an invasion in their life.

Morning came, and they both had some ideas about who to ask about what had been going on while they were away. Phillip would ask the local guy who shoveled snow for him if he had seen any tracks on the property when he came to plough. Marilee would contact Jeannie next door as she was in and out a lot and was always quite observant about things going on in the neighborhood. They hoped they would find an answer today.

Marilee was finally able to catch Jeannie at home shortly after lunch, and when she heard what had happened, she came right over. She had not seen anyone around the house except the snow plough company, so she thought that during the daytime, no one had tried to get in. She couldn't vouch for the overnight periods. Marilee had not told Jeannie about her hope of finding information inside the doll but had to explain now why she really needed to find the doll.

Jeannie's interest was really piqued now, so Marilee had to tell her about the letter from the dumbwaiter as well and that she hoped there were more letters inside the doll to reveal who the letter and the clothing belonged to. Jeannie was speechless, which didn't happen often, but really didn't have any solution to the mystery. She did say she would help Marilee in any way she could and that maybe Donna would have an idea or might have heard of a similar case at the museum. She also asked Marilee if she had seen or heard any ghosts in the house. When she saw the look on Marilee's face, she knew the answer. Marilee had not told anyone except Phillip about her dreams, but now she decided she had to share them with Jeannie. After relating all the dreams about the crying, whistling, and sobbing she heard and the noises in the attic, Jeannie said she was not surprised. The former owner had once confided to Jeannie that she thought the house was haunted but did not want anyone to know. Jeannie went on to say that most houses in this area were haunted as most homes had someone die in the home due to tragic circumstances or natural causes. Marilee was surprised but not greatly as she had suspected this to be the case. What she really wanted to know was who the person in the attic was, and why they were there. She wouldn't have any answers today, but she was sure the missing doll held some clues.

MARCH

The month of March came in like a lion with another serious snowstorm. The snow was wet and caused numerous branches to fall on wires, leaving a large part of the area without power for two and a half days. People were keeping warm by using fireplaces but only if they didn't have electric starters. Many others moved in with friends and relatives until power was restored. Phillip and Marilee were lucky enough to have three fireplaces that kept the house warm enough so pipes didn't freeze, and they had a gas range, allowing them to cook meals. They also invited Jeannie and her husband and Donna and her husband to stay with them as their homes were totally dependent upon electricity. It was a bit like an extended party as the two couples had brought food from their refrigerators and freezers with them. Phillip had also rigged up a generator he had so their refrigerator and freezer would run enough to keep food from spoiling. Fortunately, it was cold enough outside to keep some food and, of course, the beer and wine cool by keeping it in the carriage house. It wasn't exactly like running the B&B as both Jeannie and Donna wanted to help cook the meals and clean up as well. Marilee was used to working alone in the kitchen, but this was sort of fun, and it would only last until the power was back on.

Between meals and without being able to do much else in the house, the talk turned to the missing doll and the possibility of the house being haunted. During daylight hours, the three women searched the rooms to see if the doll had turned up or been missed in the last search. Of course, nothing was found. They discussed the history of the house, and knowing to whom the land had been deeded, they figured they knew who the family was. Also, the monogrammed linens found in the trunk probably did belong to the Van Everys. Of course, without power, no one could go on the internet to search the family tree.

The men would make occasional trips to the other houses, making sure nothing was freezing. They did have to drain a few tanks so toilets wouldn't freeze, but they seemed to be enjoying this short time roughing it. It was also their job to keep the fireplaces burning, and this was a nonstop effort to keep the wood supplied.

The third night at dinner, the candles were all lit, and a lovely meal was being eaten in the dining room. Suddenly, there was a noise that sounded like a motor running. No one could identify it until Phillip walked to the kitchen and realized it was the refrigerator running without the help of the generator. He went over and flipped the light switch to discover the power was back on. They had become so used to candlelight and quietness that the noise of an appliance almost seemed like an intrusion. The group decided to finish dinner by candlelight before returning to the modern world. After dinner, the friends gathered their belongings and returned home but agreed to meet again when the next big power outage occurred.

Marilee and Phillip cleaned up after dinner, turned off lights that were on, and disconnected the appliances from the generator. The temperature had warmed up significantly, and it actually felt spring-like outside. It had been three days of entertaining, so both Phillip and Marilee were ready for a good night's sleep in a warm house tonight. They did not have to worry about pipes freezing or fireplaces burning safely.

Phillip fell asleep immediately, but Marilee was still thinking about the doll. Suddenly, she began to hear the sobbing again, but this time, she was in a bedroom watching a young girl reading.

News from Across the River

Hannah had hurried back to the house after Peter had left and went back to bed. She dared not light any lamps as someone might come in to see what was wrong. She desperately wanted to read the letter but could not see in the dark. It would have to wait until daylight. She tried to sleep but could not, so she held the letter close to her and waited in the dark until the first bit of light started to show through her window. She silently crept to the window seat and opened the curtains just enough to be able to see the writing.

Dear Hannah,

I love you so much and want to be with you forever. I must go with my parents at this time, or I will never see them again, and I am worried that I might be considered the enemy because of my parent's beliefs. I really do not care about this war and want to stay here on the farm. Please forgive my parents for their thinking, and remember that I love you. Maybe this war will end very soon, and I can return. I do not think my parents will ever return to this area again, but as soon as it is possible, I will return. My Father has not sold the farm but has asked the neighbor to the south to continue working it until further notice. He is a good man and will not take advantage of the situation. Maybe when I come back, I can take over the farm, and we can live there and raise our family. I want to be with you forever. On the last page, I have written a letter to your father, asking for his permission to marry you. Please give this to him when you think the time is right. If you wait until the soldiers decide there is no need for war, he may be happier about us getting married. Right now, everyone is very angry and seem to be on opposite sides. I hope and pray that everyone will be calm and there will be no war. Please remember to find a safe hiding place for these letters as I do not want you to get into trouble because of my writing to you. We will meet again on the fifth day of June at your dock at midnight. We will use the same code to let each other know we are there. Remember to only wait in hiding for half an hour. I will try my best to come, but the situation may change, and it may be too dangerous. Please be safe while you wait. I have enclosed a small coin that I found once and would like this to be a token of my love for you while we are apart. I love you so much, Hannah, and I cherish all the times we have been able to be together. Please remember me always.

Love forever,
Peter

Hannah held the paper to her chest and thought she might as well be dead. How was she ever going to be able to carry on around the house, knowing that Peter might never return? She knew he was being optimistic about the war, but having heard her brothers and her father talk, she knew there would be a war, and it would probably last a long time. Hannah knew she should not read the letter from Peter, asking for her hand in marriage, but she just needed to read more of Peter's writing. It seemed as though he was closer when she read his letters.

Dear Mr. Van Every,

I am writing this letter to ask for your permission to marry your daughter Hannah. Even though my parents do not agree that the British should retain this part of the country, I do feel close to the British way of life. I have had to accompany my parents across the river as I am still considered a minor and must obey my parents. When this war is over, I shall return, and I would like to marry Hannah with your blessing. I am hoping to establish a farm in the area so I can support your daughter, and we can raise a family.

Yours Sincerely,
Peter Gillham

Now Hannah was weeping silently. It was almost time to get up for the day, and she had no idea how she would be able to talk to anyone or do her chores. She found the coin in the bottom of the envelope and decided it would fit in her locket. That way, she could have it with her always. Hannah began to get dressed. She tried to wash the red from her eyes but was not very successful. She put the letters in her work pocket for now and tied it around her waist. Later, she would look for a safe place. Now, she had to go down for breakfast, but really she just wanted to stay in her room and cry. Just as she opened the door to leave, her mother walked by and saw how sad Hannah looked. Hannah immediately broke into tears and fell into her mother's arms. Mrs. Van Every half-carried Hannah back into the room, thinking she was ill. Hannah then told her how sad she was as Peter and his family were leaving. She told her mother she liked Peter, and Mrs. Van Every said she thought that might be the case. Hannah did not tell her mother that Peter had asked her to marry him or about the letters and the future meetings. She knew her mother would be angry and forbid it. Her mother tried to tell her that maybe the war would be over soon, just as Peter had said, but Hannah wasn't so sure. She felt a bit better as now she had shared part of the news with someone, but it still seemed a long time until June fifth, when she would see Peter again.

* * *

Suddenly, Marilee realized it was morning, and she was alone in bed. Where was Phillip and what time was it? She sat up, looked at the clock, and saw it was after eight. She must have really gone to sleep after dreaming about the girl again. She felt refreshed but somehow a bit sad as though someone had gone away and might not return. These dreams were starting to influence her life. She went downstairs and found Phillip reading the paper and drinking coffee, just like he always did. That part was very reassuring. Phillip had gathered all the candles from the rooms and brought them to the kitchen. That had been an interesting three-day adventure reminiscent of another time period. Marilee knew she had a bit of cleaning up to do as the laundry and cleaning had been ignored during the power outage.

Today would be a cleaning day, and maybe there would be time to look for the doll.

March continued to be cool for a week and then, as if someone had waved a wand, the weather changed. A warm breeze began to blow up from the south, the snow melted even in the shady corners, and birds were singing. Within a week, the forsythias were a brilliant yellow, and the magnolia blossoms were ready to pop. The front lawn was covered in snow drops, and daffodils and tulips were peaking out of the soil in the gardens. This was a beautiful season, and everyone was ready for the change. The best part was that the lovely weather just made everyone feel happy. People started phoning Loyalist House to make reservations for later in the spring and early summer. Marilee and Phillip were really enjoying watching their spring garden come to life as it had been summer when they had purchased the house, so they had not seen the spring blooms.

It also gave people spring-cleaning fever, including Marilee. She felt she needed to start polishing everything in the house to be ready for their first guest of the season. March may have come in like a lion, but it certainly went out like a lamb.

APRIL

Loyalist House had its first guests of the season booked for the second week of April. The following week was Easter weekend, and all the rooms were booked for four nights. The season seemed to be starting well. Marilee was somewhat behind in her self-imposed cleaning schedule due to all the interruptions that had happened during March. She still had not found the doll, and this really bothered her as she felt it was the best clue she had had to finding out about the noises in the attic and the letter found in the dumbwaiter. She planned to have all the rooms ready by the Thursday before the guests were to arrive, and that would give her a whole day to look for the doll. She could not remember if she had looked in all the containers and cupboards in the attic, so that would be her next step. For now, she would begin scrubbing all the surfaces and washing all the linens.

It was exciting to be reassembling each room with decor that was planned last year. She had found a few new accessories while in Florida to use in the rooms and decided to remove one for each added. This way, the rooms would not become overloaded with unnecessary trinkets. It was important to have only one focal point in the room so the guests would feel relaxed and calm. The week went quickly, and each night, both Marilee and Phillip had fallen into bed, ready for sleep. Phillip had been working on small repairs and paint touch-ups as well as outdoor jobs. There were no dreams this week at all for Marilee, and she was a bit disappointed as it was like reading a book and looking forward to the next chapter. By Wednesday, Marilee had everything ready and was waiting for the town inspectors to come and check out the B&B for fire safety and compliance with local bylaws. This was an annual event, and any infraction could delay your license being granted.

The bylaw officer arrived right on time at ten and asked first to see how Loyalist House kept records of their guests. Marilee and Phillip had been warned by a friend that this was very important to the bylaw officer, so they had kept very good records of names, addresses, and even car license plate numbers. No one was really sure why this was important, but there were rumors of B&B owners operating more rooms than their license allowed. Loyalist House was licensed to operate up to seven rooms, and they really only had five, so they were not worried but kept records all the same.

Of course, he had to see each room, and he walked through hallways and insisted that each door be opened to make sure it was as they said and not another hidden room. He really was an untrusting soul. Marilee really wanted to say that they rented out the closet on busy nights but knew that would only get her into trouble. When they came to the attic door, he asked where it went, and when Marilee said only to the attic, he looked at her and said he had to see for himself. Up they went, and when he saw a sitting area with a day bed and a play area, he asked where the bathroom was, and who used this room. Again, Marilee wanted to say that ghosts didn't need bathrooms but were happy with quiet spaces, but she said it was only used by family as a quiet getaway to read and relax. The bylaw officer was very concerned about the bed and told them he was marking it down on their application and that the bed must be removed so it could not be used as a bedroom. He reminded them that all bedrooms must have a bathroom on the same floor available to the guests using that room. He said that someone would be back in a week to see if the bed had been removed before their license could be granted. Phillip was steaming but kept his cool as this guy knew he had the power of the moment. After a tour of the house, he wanted to see the area for guest parking. When applying for a license, B&B owners had to include a scale drawing of the property with the location of all buildings and dimensions of easements, property lines, and parking areas. This had been done, but the bylaw officer was the final authority on the accuracy of the drawing. Apparently, he could tell distances by just looking at the space. Marilee looked at Phillip and hoped he wouldn't explode and also hoped this man would leave quickly before either of them said something to jeopardize their application.

Now that the inspection was over, the bylaw officer seemed to take on another personality as he began to chat about insignificant things. They couldn't believe it and didn't really want to have a friendly conversation with him as they were quite annoyed with his attitude. Fortunately, the fire inspector drove in the driveway at that moment, so they were able to say good-bye after arranging for him to return on Friday to see that the bed was taken out of the attic.

The fire inspector introduced himself as Ted and was as positive about everything as the bylaw officer had been negative. *How refreshing,* thought Marilee. He explained he had to check all the smoke detectors and fire extinguishers in the home, and after locating them, he would be testing each one to make sure it worked properly.

Ted then started at the top floor and pushed the smoke detector and then proceeded to run down the stairs to check if each detector on each floor was ringing including the basement. Since he had worked his way down, it meant he also had to run back up to the upper completed floors to see if they worked as well. The whole procedure took forty minutes and involved forty minutes of Ted running up and down the stairs while the alarm was ringing nonstop. If he did this all day, he would never have to go to the gym and work out. Also, Marilee thought that would be a good way to be able to eat all the chocolate you wanted and never gain weight. He did sit down at the end and accepted a drink of water as he explained what he would write in the report. Loyalist House had passed the fire inspections with flying colors.

Ted talked for a bit, probably to get his heart rate down, and then he was off. That inspection had been almost enjoyable except for the noise. Marilee and Phillip were still somewhat upset with their treatment by the bylaw officer. Marilee decided she would talk to her friend Jeannie as she seemed to know everyone in town. Maybe she knew a reason he was so negative.

The rest of the day was uneventful, and Marilee managed to get everything ready, including the grocery shopping by dinner time, and Phillip asked a friend to help carry the bed from the attic to the office area of the owner's quarters. They would make room for it there and might even move it back to the attic later in the summer as they knew no one but family were ever up there.

The next morning, Marilee was awake early and ready to begin the search for the doll. She would start in the attic and look in all the containers, even though she knew she hadn't put it there. After breakfast, she took her second cup of coffee up to the attic and began the search. The plastic containers all had the toys in them, just as she had left them. Next, she went to the dresser and checked the drawers. Only extra linens were stored there, and she thought maybe they should be downstairs in the linen closet. She soon had a pile of things to carry down the stairs. This was a good exercise and a way to keep from accumulating an excess of household goods.

Finally, there was only the trunk left to open, and she was sure it wasn't in there, but Marilee opened it anyway. The boys clothes that had been around the doll were rolled up in the bottom of the trunk, but they somehow looked larger than before. Marilee lifted it out and unrolled it. Suddenly, she began to feel chills running through her body. The doll was rolled up in the clothes just as it had been when she had found it the first time. Marilee put it down and went to the stairs to call Phillip. He came running as she sounded alarmed. Marilee showed Phillip the clothes and the doll in the trunk. She knew she had not put it there, and Phillip said he had not done it either. This was a puzzle. If someone had been in the house when they were away, why would they hide the doll, how did they know where to hide it, and why would they not have just taken it if it was valuable? None of this made sense. They both looked at each other, and the same thought was running through their minds. What if they really did have a ghost in the attic?

The cell phone Marilee had with her rang, and they both jumped and grabbed each other and then laughed. Ghosts didn't use cell phones. It was the B&B booking service calling and had a guest looking for accommodation tonight for one night only and wanted to be along the river. Marilee suddenly became suspicious about why this person wanted to stay at their place. And was it just a coincidence that they had called at just that moment? She did question the agency a bit more and decided it would be OK. Of course, that meant she would have to leave the doll and its contents until another time. Right now, she had to go and start some baking. They decided to wrap the doll back in the clothes and put it in the trunk. Maybe this move wouldn't anger the ghost, if they had one, and they would know where to look in a few days. She had to stop thinking about this, so she started deciding on what to bake. Maybe hot cross buns would be good for breakfast.

The guests arrived at Loyalist House about an hour after the phone call. Marilee didn't really like check-ins before four in the afternoon, but as everything was ready and since there was only one couple, she would let it happen today. Mr. and Mrs. Thompson seemed very nice and told Phillip and Marilee they were researching their family tree. They had some information about their ancestors and felt that it was in this area that they had resided when they had come as refugees in the late 1700s. They were hoping to talk to some locals who might be able to help them. Marilee explained about their move to the house less than a year ago but told them about all the records at the museum that might be of some help. They also had several places they wanted to visit, including cemeteries and churches, after lunch. Marilee showed them to their room, all the while retelling what she knew of the history of the house. They seemed very interested and suggested that maybe they could visit after they returned from dinner tonight. Marilee said that would be fine. Within ten minutes, they were off on their adventure to find their ancestors.

Marilee spent the rest of the day baking and preparing for breakfast but not really accomplishing much else. Her thoughts were really on the attic. She was somewhat interested in the Thompson's story as somewhere she had read that there was a descendant of Van Every's by that name. Marilee had found a copy of the family history at the library, and she had made a copy to bring home. It was in the living room along with other interesting articles for the guests to read. She would point it out to the Thompsons this evening.

Mr. and Mrs. Thompson arrived back at Loyalist House shortly before seven and were sitting in the living room when Marilee came out to the front of the house. Marilee had left the family story on the table, and they were studying it. Apparently, their relatives had settled in this area but with a different spelling of their surname. The Thomson who was related to the Van Every had no "p" in their surname. They seemed a bit disappointed and said it would have been lovely to have this house and the ancestors as part of their family tree. They had visited several places and found out nothing but had enjoyed their day. They decided that even if they never discovered who their ancestors were, they might still come back to visit and stay at Loyalist House. The rest of the evening was spent chatting about a variety of topics, and by nine, this enjoyable couple said goodnight and retired to their room.

Breakfast was easy with only one couple, and the food served was appreciated. The hot cross buns were delicious, and the extras and a recipe card were sent home with the Thompsons. As Marilee was cleaning up, she was actually glad the season had begun. She had missed the guests and the interesting bits of information they all brought to Loyalist House. Tonight, all five rooms would be full, and even though the bylaw officer had not returned to see that the bed had been removed, they decided that not having confirmation of their license was merely a formality. Within the hour, there was a knock at the door, and a young man said he was with the town and was here to check on the anomalies associated with their B&B license. He was very polite and asked if they had removed the bed. Marilee said yes and asked him to follow her to the attic so he could see. He said it wouldn't be necessary, initialed the box, asked her to sign, and gave her a copy. He said this would serve as their temporary license until the official one could be mailed. Marilee was speechless and thought, *what a breath of fresh air!* Maybe he could pass some of his people skills on to the other bylaw officer. She thanked him, and he was off. They were legally a B&B again for another year.

Later that afternoon, the guests started arriving. The first to arrive were two couples who had come together from a northern US state. They were pleasant and chatty and thrilled with the charm of Loyalist House. They said they would eat anything Marilee made as a friend had recommended this B&B and said the food was delicious. These were ideal guests. About an hour later, the next two couples arrived together, and they were from the Toronto area. Though not as chatty, they were very polite and seemed to like their rooms but were not as easy to read as the first group. The last couple did not arrive until a few hours past dinner. They were very quiet and would hardly answer the questions about breakfast choices. Marilee and Phillip wondered how the other two groups would interact with these people and hoped they would not be excluded from any conversations at breakfast. Maybe they were just tired as they had driven for over six hours to get here. There wasn't much she could do at this moment, and Marilee had no intention of doing personality profiles of the guests to see if they were compatible. In the end, it always seemed to work out that everyone enjoyed each other's company after they had relaxed a bit. In the meantime, Marilee began preparing strawberry French toast for breakfast. This was one of those recipes that could be changed to accommodate any fruit that was in season.

The rest of the evening passed quickly as Marilee and Phillip completed all the night-before preparations for breakfast. The guests all came in at various times and went directly to their rooms. By ten, it was quiet, and all the upstairs lights were out. These were tired guests, but that usually meant they were early risers. Marilee and Phillip decided to go to bed early for a change as it had been a hectic few weeks. Marilee was thinking about what types of jam to serve with the muffins, when she heard someone humming a tune that she thought she knew but couldn't quite remember the words. It might have been a children's song.

The Hiding Spot

Hannah decided she must find a place to hide Peter's letters. She had promised Peter she would so no one could find them. She searched around her room, but every place she thought of could be discovered either by her mother or her younger sister.

Hannah's parents were, by standards at the time, quite wealthy. They owned a large amount of land and farmed it but had many people working for them. They also owned several slaves who lived on the property and worked in the fields. In the house, Hannah's mother ran the household, but there was a cook and a housekeeper who helped clean and do household chores. Hannah was expected to keep her room tidy and help around the house, but unlike many girls her age, she did have time read and play the piano. She did not attend school, but her mother taught her to read and learn about gardening and to do needlework. Her mother also taught her to play the piano as the family was lucky enough to own one. Hannah was being educated to be a lady, and that was rare in this part of the world. Most girls had to either work in the fields or the house or take care of younger siblings as pioneer life was difficult.

As Hannah was searching her room, she thought of the trunk or under the bed, but those spots did not seem safe enough. She might wrap them in a blanket, but where would she put it? She had asked for a box to keep her treasures for Christmas, but she had not received one, and it was a long time before her birthday. There must be something she could put the letters in. Suddenly, she heard footsteps coming down the hall, and her mother was calling her. Hannah turned quickly and, in her haste, knocked her doll off the chair and onto the floor. The poor doll had lost her wig, and her head was dangling to one side. Quickly, Hannah shoved both the doll and the letters under the bed. She would retrieve them later and somehow reattach the head back on to the doll. It had been her favorite doll and was well-loved when Hannah had been little. She didn't play with it now but used it as a decoration in her room. Suddenly, she had an idea, but it would have to wait as her mother opened the door.

*   *   *

Marilee awoke with a start. She was thinking about the doll in the attic, but she couldn't recall what had triggered the thought. She looked at the clock, and it was almost seven. She had better get up and start breakfast. Phillip was already in the kitchen, beginning the bacon. The coffee was made, and he had oatmeal simmering on the stove for himself and Marilee. How could she ever manage without him! Together, they had their breakfast before any guests arrived in the dining room. It was always nice when they could sit for at least twenty minutes and enjoy their breakfast.

Breakfast had been arranged for eight thirty, and all the couples were very prompt. At first, it was very quiet. Everyone was being polite, and just the niceties were exchanged. Phillip took the coffee pot in for refills and asked a general question about a current political figure in the news for all the wrong reasons. Suddenly, several people had opinions, and the conversation began. Phillip did not stay to take part but returned to the kitchen while the discussion continued in the dining room. If conversation died down again, he would go back in with another somewhat controversial topic. He read the paper every morning, so he always had a lot of current topics to throw out for discussion. It usually took only one or two and then the group began to feel comfortable enough with each other that they were never at a loss for things to talk about.

Marilee's worries about the quiet couple being left out of the conversation were unfounded as they discovered they had mutual friends living in the same town. It always amazed Marilee that this happened so often. After breakfast, they all took more coffee out on the front porch to continue their visiting. The weather had turned wonderful, and as the house faced east, the sun shining on the porch made it warm enough to think it was summer.

Marilee cleaned the kitchen and was planning her day. It shouldn't take too much time to tidy up the rooms as these guests would be here for three more nights. Tomorrow would take longer as it meant changing all the beds. It seemed like her main thoughts lately were always about having enough time to go and check the doll, but it never seemed to happen. Today, she knew she must check the doll and see what was inside. As she went about cleaning and tidying the house, she heard sirens close enough to be just at their driveway. Marilee hurried to the front porch and joined their guests as well as Phillip. Two police cars roared by but slowed just past their driveway. They were quickly followed by several fire trucks.

This looked serious, so the group walked to the road and continued along to where the emergency vehicles had stopped. There was a car dangling over the edge of the bank, looking as though it could fall at any moment down the thirty feet to the river. Someone must have been speeding along the twisty road and lost control on the curve. There was a lot of shouting and men carrying ropes and equipment, and it look like mass confusion, but within fifteen minutes, the car was secure and being dragged back to solid ground. Now, the emergency workers could concentrate on helping the occupants of the car. It was soon revealed that the driver was an elderly gentleman and had suffered some sort of a physical seizure, causing him to steer the car off the road. His passenger was also elderly and though conscious, very upset. She must have been the wife. There was only one ambulance on the scene, and the paramedics would not allow the wife to travel with her husband to the hospital. Marilee quickly stepped in and told the police she lived across the road, and the woman was more than welcome to wait at their home until another ambulance arrived. At that point, the paramedics decided the woman was not injured enough to warrant an ambulance and would have to find her own way to the hospital. Everyone in the group of visitors was appalled at the lack of compassion for this woman. The police seemed to accept this procedure as normal, much to everyone's surprise. Phillip asked which hospital they were going to and said he would drive her there. He quickly went back to the house, grabbed Marilee's purse, and returned with the car. Marilee and Phillip helped the woman find her purse and a jacket, and she got in the car with them to travel to the hospital. The guests said they would lock up the house, and the police said they would be in touch with the hospital about where the car was being towed. This had all taken place within forty-five minutes, but it seemed like hours.

On the way to the hospital, the woman told them her name was Martha Morris, and she and her husband were visiting the area for the weekend. They were to stay at a small B&B in town, but she couldn't remember the name. Marilee said not to worry as they often had e-mails from the booking groups trying to find the place visitors had booked but had forgotten their booking information. Phillip said he would find out for her and let the owners know what had happened.

They arrived at the hospital and found Martha's husband in the emergency department. By this time, he was conscious but had no recollection of the accident. Now, the waiting would begin as the hospital was already busy with several people on stretchers and others waiting in chairs. Martha stayed with her husband, Frank, while Phillip and Marilee began to solve the B&B mystery. As there were over two hundred B&B's in town, it could take a while. They phoned their friend Gail at the booking agency, and she said she would check records and make as many calls as it took to find the right B&B. There were lots of B&B's, but it was still a closely connected group who knew other members in the association.

Marilee decided that Martha and Frank's family needed to be contacted, so she found out the names and called the son and daughter. Fortunately, they were home and did not live too far away. Both would leave immediately to come and be with their parents. By this time, Frank had been seen by a Doctor, and they were doing some tests. Marilee stayed with Martha while they waited. She noticed several people walking by, looking at her oddly, so she patted her hair to make sure it wasn't standing on end. She knew she had no lipstick on, but that shouldn't matter. Martha saw her puzzled look and asked why she was wearing an apron that said "Keep your eggs sunny side up." Marilee realized she had forgotten to take her apron off before she had left the house. Marilee explained to Martha that they ran a B&B, and she had just finished serving breakfast. The apron was one she had received at a trade show and always amused her guests at breakfast. They had a small chuckle about it, and Marilee took it off and put it in her purse. Marilee tried to keep Martha chatting about herself and her family to keep her busy while they waited. At this point, Marilee sent Phillip home and said she would wait until Martha's family arrived. She would call Phillip at that point, and he could drive back to get her.

Marilee and Martha changed rooms three or four times when Frank would return from tests. Finally, after three hours, Frank was admitted and in a room. Finally their children arrived and the story was retold about driving off the road. No one had yet diagnosed Frank's medical issue. Marilee decided she was no longer needed and phoned Phillip to come. Martha's son thanked Marilee for staying with his mother, took her business card from the B&B, and gave her his. He said he would call her to let her know how Frank was doing. It seemed strange just to walk out and leave this family as she felt she knew them well now. Marilee said they had guests for the next few days, but if they needed a place to stay, she would try and find them a spot. Phillip arrived and had the name of the B&B Frank and Martha had booked and the place where their car was taken. Goodbyes were said, and Phillip and Marilee left to go home. Marilee was exhausted and starving, so they stopped and picked up lunch on the way back to Loyalist House. Of course, by this time, it was almost supper, and even though she just wanted to sleep, she knew she had some baking to do as well as finish cleaning. What a surprise to find her kitchen totally clean, the beds all made, and the towels gathered in the laundry room! She began thanking Phillip, but he said that when he had returned home, it was like that. The guests had decided to help out. These were the best guests ever! Now, Marilee could lie down for just an hour and do the baking later.

Her head barely hit the pillow, and she was suddenly transported to a bedroom where a young girl was sitting on the floor, holding a doll.

Hiding the Letters

Hannah felt bad that her doll's head had fallen off. It had been her favorite toy to play with when she was little. She picked up the doll's head and looked inside. It was hollow but certainly not big enough to hold all the letters she wanted to hide. She picked up the body and saw that it had stuffing of some sort to make the body firm but still soft enough to cuddle. Hannah picked at a bit of the stuffing, and some of it came out in a chunk in her hand. She had an idea. She went across the room and found her knitting basket. There, she found a needle that would loosen the stuffing. She would take out just enough to create a space for the letters. If she folded them and then rolled them up very tightly, they would fit inside, and no one would think to look inside a doll. The task took some time, but finally, the letters were safely inside. It made her a bit sad though since Hannah liked to read them at night as it made her feel as though Peter was with her.

Now she must figure out a way to reattach the head. She found a large wool needle, and with a piece of yarn from her knitting basket, she carefully sewed the head back on to the doll. The head still flopped a bit to one side, and you could see the stitching. This would be a sure give away that something was inside. Hannah then remembered that she had begun to knit a scarf that she might need next winter. Digging to the bottom of the knitting basket, she discovered it was still there, waiting to be finished. It would take too long to finish it, so she kept digging through the basket. Right at the bottom, she found a piece of black velvet ribbon she had been saving for something. This would make a perfect chocker around the doll's neck. It took only about another twenty minutes to secure the ribbon in place so it would not slip and reveal the stitches holding the head in place. It looked just like something a young girl might do when she was playing with her doll. The velvet ribbon did look slightly out of place on a doll dressed in a fine cotton baby dress, but it would have to do. At least now the doll's head stayed straight up, and you could not see the loose stitches holding it on. For now, she would put the doll in her knitting basket until she thought of a better place to hide it. Hannah piled the extra yarn on top of the basket, stuck the needles into the wool, and put the basket back in the corner of her room. She could now say she had carried out her promise to Peter to hide their letters in a safe spot.

* * *

Marilee woke up with a start. She knew what was inside the doll. Of course, once again, this would not be the day to find them as it was almost dinner time, and she had done no baking for tomorrow. She quickly went down to the kitchen and began to make strawberry almond muffins for breakfast. She also began to whip up a batch of savory scones. Her mind kept repeating "look inside the doll" while she worked. Of course, she mismeasured the baking powder for the muffins, and they all turned out looking like peaked mountains, ready to erupt. She tasted one, and they tasted fine, so she decided to improvise and drizzled a glaze of icing sugar and water over the top and called it snow on the mountain muffins. She tried to concentrate more while making the scones. She wanted to call Jeannie and ask her over so they could look inside the doll together. To give herself extra time tonight, she decided to make eggs benedict with Canadian bacon tomorrow morning. These, of course, all had to be made just before serving.

She called Jeannie while the scones were baking, and Jeannie arranged to meet her at ten thirty the next morning. It would be a long night! Marilee thought this was silly; she should just go and look inside the doll herself. But something was stopping her. She was afraid that either she would find nothing significant, or she would find something that relayed a sad story.

Marilee finished her baking, made sure she had all the ingredients for breakfast, and then managed to put together a dinner for herself and Phillip that was relatively nutritious. At dinner, she told Phillip about her dream and about what she thought was inside the doll. He didn't seem to be as excited about this whole story as she was. He was concerned that if they found out the house was haunted, their business might suffer.

Marilee was so keyed up about the doll that she didn't sleep well all night. By morning, she was ready to sleep but had to get up for breakfast. She remembered seeing the hands on the clock pass every hour during the night. This would be a long day.

The good thing about making poached eggs was that they could be made ahead of time and kept in ice water until it was time for serving. Then you just had to pop them into boiling water for about thirty seconds to bring them back up to eating temperature. Marilee had learned this trick from a chef friend who worked at a large hotel. It all made sense, especially if you were making eggs benedict for five hundred people. Of course, this trick worked really well for ten people as well. The hollandaise sauce turned out nicely this morning and did not curdle as it was prone to do sometimes. Marilee also knew a trick to fix that problem but did not need to use it this morning.

The guests arrived in the dining room, and all were curious about the couple who had been in the accident yesterday. Phillip had contacted the family and was told that the gentleman who had been driving had suffered a heart attack but was stable and would be fine in time. Their car, unfortunately, did not fare as well.

Phillip served the fruit parfaits and placed the muffins and scones on the table. It always amazed Phillip and Marilee how easily impressed their guest were with simple things such as the parfaits. Also, the less-than-perfect muffins with some icing and a new name were a hit today. Those muffins would not have won any prizes at a fair due to their shape.

Breakfast went well, everyone loved the eggs benedict, and as they all had plans for the day, the guests were anxious to leave.

Marilee quickly tidied up, and as soon as every room was vacant, she began the task of changing the sheets and cleaning the rooms so they would look fresh when the guests returned. Before she was finished, the doorbell rang, and Jeannie was there, ready for their adventure. She helped Marilee finish up the last room, and off they went to the attic.

Once in the attic, they began to open the trunk. Marilee hoped the doll had not been moved again by whomever or whatever did it the last time. The trunk lid opened, and there, right on top, was the doll, still wrapped in the old clothes. Marilee picked up the doll and then began to remove the ribbon from around the neck of the doll. She was wondering why she had not done this before. Just as she had seen in the dream, there were loose wool stitches holding the head on to the body of the doll. Jeannie had brought scissors with her, so she offered them to Marilee to cut the stitches. Once this was done, the head literally fell off in their hands, and the rolled up papers inside the doll were within reach.

Jeannie held the doll as Marilee gently pulled the papers from the doll's body. The papers were old, yellowed, and somewhat brittle, so they had to unroll them gently. Once opened, they saw there were six pages. Some had been written on both horizontally and vertically, so they were hard to read. Marilee and Jeannie laid the papers on a flat surface to see if there was an order to them. It seemed that they were letters written to someone, and the writer had been very careful to include all the proper parts required in formal letter writing. No one wrote any kind of letters these days, let alone a proper formal letter. The dates indicated they were written during the summer of 1812. The material seemed to be familiar to Marilee, and she then realized it was part of the dreams she had been having. This was unreal for Marilee. She did not know why she was chosen to have these dreams and why she now had the doll and the letters. What was she to do with all this information?

First, she would have to find out who wrote these letters and then she could figure out the whys. Marilee suggested they take the letters and the doll downstairs to decide how they were going to solve this mystery. Marilee picked up the other letter they had found in the dumbwaiter, grabbed some extra plastic sleeves, and they headed down to the kitchen. She placed each page in a protective sleeve so they could be handled and then made a pot of coffee as this could be a long afternoon.

Marilee and Jeannie discovered the writers were people named Hannah and Peter, but no surnames were given. It seemed as though the two writers were in love but unable to see each other due to family conflicts. War was mentioned as was taking sides and seemed to be taking place during the war of 1812. Marilee also told Jeannie about all her dreams and what she saw, and they seemed to be a reflection of the letters. Had these two lovers lived near Loyalist House? Was Loyalist House the home of one of the lovers? Marilee knew the names of the occupants of Loyalist House when it had been built, so she decided to compare names with the history she had had reprinted from the museum.

She reread the history and found that the original owner's name was Van Every, and the second generation had had a daughter named Hannah. It didn't give any other information about her age, but it was noted she was not listed as residing there with the third generation of the Every's. Possibly, this story had a happy ending, and she and Peter did get married and lived somewhere else. This scenario, of course, did not explain the suspicion of the ghost in the attic. Every time Marilee thought she was getting closer to an answer, more questions always arose.

After discussing the many possibilities all afternoon, Marilee and Jeannie decided to do some more research at the museum to find out about other families in the area. They arranged to meet the next day after lunch. By then, Marilee's guests would be gone, and she would have more time to devote to this new project.

The two weeks flew by as Marilee spent most of her spare time at the museum, researching the early families living in this area. The few guests that did come to stay at Loyalist House were easy to entertain. They all had their own agenda of activities and loved any of the breakfasts Marilee cooked. Before she knew it, April was over, and she still had not solved the mystery.

MAY

May was a beautiful month. The blossoms were at their best, and driving through the countryside looked like you were in the middle of white or pink clouds. If you stopped at the side of the road, there was a fragrance in the air that ought to be bottled and sold. The birds were singing, the bees were buzzing, and everyone was in a good mood. Of course, this beauty was one of the things that brought tourists to the area. Out of the thirty-one days in May, Marilee and Phillip had guests coming in on twenty-eight. Not all the rooms were booked, but they were going to be very busy. About half of the guests booked were repeats who had been coming to Loyalist House for at least two years. Marilee and Phillip had not met these people, but it would be interesting to see if they booked again for next year, now that it was under new ownership.

Marilee needed to redo her menus so they reflected spring instead of winter. It would be nice to use asparagus, wild leeks, and rhubarb in her recipes. She loved this season as well as summer since all the fresh fruit available for cooking was so accessible in this area.

Marilee had discovered there was a rhubarb patch near the dock down by the river, and the last time she had checked it, the rhubarb was almost ready for cutting. Tomorrow morning's muffins would be rhubarb-pecan muffins.

Today, there were three groups checking in, so along with the muffins and fruit parfaits, an asparagus quiche would be nice for breakfast. Marilee walked down to the river to cut the rhubarb for the muffins. As she was pulling the stalks apart to see where to cut, a piece of bronze metal caught her eye. It was probably just a nail or screw, but Marilee scraped the earth from around it and picked it up. It looked like a coin but was definitely not one from recent days. She did not recognize any of the imprints on it, and much of it was still caked in mud, so the words were not legible. Phillip might be interested in it, so she put it in her pocket and continued cutting stalks of rhubarb. By the time she finished cutting, there was enough to make several batches of muffins and a pie.

Marilee returned to the house and began cleaning and cutting the rhubarb and put it in the pot to stew. She also packaged up several bags that each held enough rhubarb to make a pie later. Phillip would be happy as this was one of his favorite pies next to blueberry, apple, peach, and cherry. Phillip actually loved all kinds of pie.

The guests all arrived at four, all within a half hour of each other. Everyone seemed pleasant, but Marilee was a bit worried when one of the women asked if the air-conditioning was on. As it was May and still not hot out, she had not turned it on yet. Marilee said she would check the temperature in the house and turn it on if needed. The temperature in the house was still below what the cool setting would be, so she just turned it on and let it come on when and if the house became hot. The couples all left for dinner and a show, and all returned close to eleven. The evening was pleasant, and Marilee and Phillip were sitting on the front porch when the guests returned for the night. Everyone had enjoyed the theatre, goodnights were said, and Marilee thought all was well. The next morning was a cool spring morning, so Marilee opened the windows to let the fresh breeze into the house. The guests came down for breakfast, and everyone loved the muffins and the quiche. They all left for various places for the day and would return just before dinner. Marilee thought this was great as she would spruce up the rooms and then do some research at the library on the Van Everys. When she entered the front room, she was horrified to see that the window was open, and there was a portable fan in it, going full blast. The room was quite cool now, but if the sun started to come in and the air-conditioning clicked on, a lot of energy would be wasted. She removed the fan and shut the window and closed the curtains to keep the sun out. Marilee also thought it must look like a one star motel with a fan blowing in an open window, and this was not the image she wanted Loyalist House to project. When she went to make up the bed, she discovered that the mattress cover had been removed from the bed and was rolled up and placed in the bottom of the closet. It, of course, had a protective layer of vinyl under the cotton pad to protect the mattress from all kinds of abuse and to keep it sanitary for all guests. It probably became too hot for this guest, so she had removed it. Marilee took a spare one from her storage cupboard and remade the bed the proper way. She could only hope it would be left on tonight. She wouldn't say anything to the guest other than that the air-conditioning was on, so the windows should be kept closed.

The next morning at breakfast, nothing was said about the bed or the window, and as they were checking out that morning, Marilee would just count it as experience. When she went to clean the rooms, she found the mattress pad still on the bed, but the bed had been made by someone other than Marilee. The guest must have removed the mattress pad and remade the bed in the morning hoping that Marilee might not notice. She decided her standards were the proper ones, and she would continue making beds the same way.

The next room she went into looked as though it had already been cleaned. The bed was made, but of course, she would have to unmake it. On the bed was a gift bag with wrapping paper coming out the top. Marilee thought her guests had forgotten part of their luggage. This had happened before, and Marilee had found pants, shoes, pillows, and books left behind. She had even phoned one guest after they had returned home to ask him to mail the key back to Loyalist House. She was pleasantly surprised when she saw her name on the bag with a thank-you note from the guests. Marilee opened the gift and found a miniature decorated Christmas tree on a platform and covered with a glass dome. These guests had obviously made this decoration. The tiny candles on the tree were very realistic. The stars were made from small buttons. Around the bottom were a miniature toy train and a teddy bear. This would be perfect to have out at Christmas for her grandchildren to see. She would phone these guests later today to thank them. These occasions always lifted Marilee's spirits and made her feel the whole business of serving guests was worthwhile. The cleaning went well the rest of the morning, and Marilee found herself whistling while she worked. By noon, she was done, except for the laundry, and since she had a day off before the next guests arrived, Marilee decided to call Jeannie and see if she would go with her to find information about the Van Every family.

Jeannie picked up Marilee after lunch, and they went to the museum first to see what they could find. They were somewhat successful but really only had the names of three generations. There was a lead, though, that could help, so they went to the Anglican Church and found records listing the christening of several Van Every babies. That probably meant the family attended church there. It would have been quite a hike in those days to travel to church along the river road from their home to town. While in the church, the gentleman who had directed them to the record books asked what they were looking for. When Marilee gave him the name, he knew where several Van Everys were buried. The plot was located out of town in a private cemetery for two families linked by marriage. There had been a visitor to the church several years ago, looking for the same names. He then kindly looked up the name in the visitor book. Marilee was able to copy the name and address of the person who might be able to help. She and Jeannie now felt they might be on the right track. They wanted to jump in the car and drive the three or four hours to talk to this couple, but sanity prevailed, and they returned home to Loyalist House to plot their next move.

The internet was a great tool, and they were able to find the name, address, and phone number of this couple. It also listed their profession. That evening, Marilee telephoned Mr. and Mrs. Thomson and explained who she was and why she was calling. Mr. Thomson was thrilled that someone would be interested in their family history. It turned out he had completed a family history and had spent time in the area documenting places and dates. He and his wife did not travel much anymore, but he would be thrilled to send her a copy of the family history. Marilee could hardly contain her enthusiasm. She told him about the letters and the doll and that maybe now she would know to whom they belonged. Mr. Thomson was also very excited, and they concluded by agreeing to keep in touch with each other as more information was discovered. As soon as Marilee hung up the phone, she told Phillip the news and then practically ran over to Jeannie's to tell her the news. Phillip said he would go with her but found he was trailing behind her all the way. Jeannie and Marilee were both talking at the same time, speculating about every detail they knew. Phillip and Ralph just watched and smiled. They decided to celebrate a small success, and so they opened a bottle of local white wine that had just been released. It met with everyone's approval, and the rest of the evening was spent talking about local issues and events that would take place this summer. As the clock struck eleven, Phillip decided it was time to go. Marilee and Jeannie would be checking the mail daily, waiting for the family history to arrive. Once Marilee was home, she was too keyed up to sleep, so she decided to bake a batch of muffins for the next few days. All the while she was baking, her thoughts were about this young girl, Hannah, in the letter and her fiancé, Peter. How would this love affair turn out? By the time the muffins were cool, Marilee was beginning to feel tired, and so she cleaned up a bit and left the dishes until morning. Phillip had already gone to bed, so she quietly crept upstairs and slipped into bed. Immediately, she fell into a deep sleep, but in the far region of her consciousness, she heard the sobbing noises. Only this time, it was from more than just one person.

News of Peter

The war had escalated, and every day, there were groups of men passing by the farm on the road. They were soldiers but were dressed in work clothes and carried guns. Often, they came to the house to ask for food. They were always given food by the cook, so there was never trouble, but Hannah's Mother was worried about her children and kept them inside most of the time, under her watchful eye. As it was summer, they had lots of food, but unless some was put away for the winter, food could soon be scarce. Often, there were British soldiers on the river in boats, patrolling for spies being sent over from the American side to check out places they could land and then attack.

Hannah hated being inside all the time, and occasionally, when her Mother was busy in the house, she slipped out to the garden to see if Joseph was there in hopes that he might have a letter for her from Peter. She always kept a watch out for soldiers approaching as she was afraid of them. Today was sunny and warm, so Hannah was walking in the garden, seeing what vegetables were ready. The beans and peas were poking through the soil as were the beets and carrots. The carrots would need thinning soon. There were lettuce and radishes ready to pick, and the potatoes were beginning to flower. The garden looked good, and the weeds had not overtaken it yet. Someone must be out here weeding. Suddenly, her heart jumped as she saw someone approaching. Hannah was about to turn and run but realized it was Joseph coming toward her. When he reached the spot where she was standing, he handed her a letter and said he had seen Peter last night on the river, and he had given this letter to be delivered to Hannah. Joseph said it was not safe to be on the river as soldiers were always watching and would shoot at anything that moved. Peter had been shot at last night but had made it safely back across the river. Joseph said he would not deliver any more letters as he was too afraid now to be down at the river at night. Hannah thanked him for the letter and said she understood. He quickly left and went back toward the barns to continue his work. Hannah slipped the letter into her pocket and returned to the house to her bedroom to read the letter. Once in her bedroom, she sat at the window and opened the letter.

Dear Hannah,

I miss you so much. Last night, I thought maybe you would see me if you were looking out your attic window. It was a full moon and very bright out. I did see Joseph, so I gave him this letter. I know I said we would meet June 5, but I don't want to wait that long. I hear the Americans are going to attack your side very soon, but I don't know where. I will be on the river again tonight if you can sneak down at midnight. Our new home is starting to look like a cabin, but we are still living in tents. Mother hates it and so do my sisters, but my Father is sure we have done the right thing. My brothers want to join the American army. I would like to come back and join the British to fight, but I would probably be considered a traitor and be shot. I will watch for you, and we will use the same signals as last time. Be careful.

All my love,
Peter.

Hannah couldn't believe it. She might see Peter tonight! It was dangerous, though, so she would need to be extra careful near the river. She went to the trunk and took out the old clothes she wore as a disguise and tucked this letter inside the doll so no one would find it. She would now go and help her Mother so she would not suspect anything. It was twelve more hours until she would see Peter. How could she wait that long!

*   *   *

Marilee awoke suddenly and discovered it was 6:00 a.m. She might as well get up. She felt as though she was forgetting something about someone but could not put her finger on what it was. There were no guests coming in until tomorrow, so today was a free day to do what she wanted. There would not be too many more free days as their bookings were increasing daily. It might be a good day to do repairs in the house and gardening outside before the busy season arrived. Marilee knew she would have to keep busy, or she would just be worrying about the arrival of the Thomson family history.

The next three days flew by with two sets of guests checking in, baking muffins and scones, and many walks to the mailbox at the end of the driveway to see if a package had arrived from Mr. Thomson. Finally, four days later, there was the long-awaited package, sitting in the mailbox with Marilee's name written in spidery handwriting on the front. This must have been an all-day task for the Thomsons, and by the looks of the handwriting, they were probably in their eighties. Marilee could hardly wait to open it but decided to call Jeannie to be with her when she did. She and Jeannie had become a team in solving this mystery. Jeannie was over in less than ten minutes, and together, they sat at the kitchen table and began to read the family history. Mr. Thomson had done a lot of research into the background of the family, all the way back to 1653. There were over two hundred pages of notes about this family, so Marilee decided to get an extra copy made, and they could each read it at their own speed. The book included some pictures of where the original homestead had been and the places members of the family had moved later. The most interesting part for Marilee and Jeannie was the inclusion of the family tree at the end of the book. It started with the family in Holland in 1653 and continued up to 1990. They quickly scanned down the generations, and bingo, there was the name Hannah that fit in the correct time frame. It was interesting that her birth date was registered, but it did not have a date for her death. It was also interesting to note that Hannah's younger sister had married a Peter Gillham in 1820. Could this be the same Peter who had written the letters to Hannah? They also confirmed that Hannah and her family were direct descendents of McGregory Van Every, the original settlers on this property. This was almost too good to be true. Now the question was, why did Hannah and Peter not marry? And why was there no date of death for Hannah? Marilee and Jeannie decided to each read the family history and maybe find the answer. Whoever found it first would call the other immediately.

The next day, Jeannie called Marilee and said she had read the whole family history and had not found any answer. Marilee had not quite finished it but had not found anything either. They decided to spend a day when neither of them was busy and try to put all the letters in chronological order, and maybe then they would be able to figure out what happened to Hannah. But the B&B season was really getting busy, and for the next two weeks, Marilee was fully booked almost every day. They finally came up with a date in early June when they could have an uninterrupted day. Until then they would try to recall even the smallest detail they may have overlooked.

Life at the B&B continued. Everyone who came was thrilled to be there and loved all the breakfasts Marilee served. Phillip was enjoying talking to guests at breakfast, and by now, he knew almost everything that was going on in the area and could discuss all kinds of facts about growing grapes and making wine. He and a friend were actually considering purchasing property and setting up a small cottage winery in the next few years. This made for wonderful conversation at breakfast as most people who visited the area were intrigued by the fact that wine could be produced in what they perceived as too far north for grape growing. Phillip loved to explain that the latitude of the area was similar to the Burgundy area of France and that because this area was between two lakes with protection from an escarpment, it made for ideal growing conditions. If any guests seemed interested and asked further questions, Phillip could go on for hours with facts and figures about climate, soil, and varieties of grapes. Marilee thought it was amusing that he had become so social and often had to go in and rescue the guests form listening to what could be called wine making 101. The guests loved the evening happy hour at Loyalist House as Phillip would always have interesting local wines to taste and could direct them to the best wineries for different wines.

Marilee had been so busy these past few weeks she had not had time to even think about Hannah and the letters. Every night, she had fallen into bed and immediately gone to sleep until the alarm went off in the morning. Now she knew why some B&B owners were so tired by the end of the season. She might have to start booking days off for sanity's sake. She was looking forward to next Wednesday when she and Jeannie would get together and talk about Hannah. Today, she would be looking for new recipes using strawberries as the local berries would be ready in a week or so.

JUNE

June was a lovely, gentle month. Peonies were in full bloom the same time as lilacs. The light breezes blowing off the lake were a bit warmer, and the scent of the flowers wafted in the air as you walked along the cobblestoned streets of Newbrook. Marilee thought about how different this town must have been two hundred years ago. It was likely there were no flowering shrubs and blooming plants except for wild ones. There would have been only mud paths for walking, and because of the dangers of war, probably no one ventured far from their home. Today, though, Marilee was walking from the museum to the post office, and it was delightful. Days like today confirmed for her that she and Phillip had made the right decision to move here. In one short year, they had become involved in many activities in the community and had made many new friends. The only thing worrying her today was not knowing what had happened to Hannah Van Every. Tomorrow, she was meeting with Jeannie, and they would see if they had missed a clue in the letters. If there were letters missing, she had no idea where they might be. She just had to get the thank-you note to Mr. and Mrs. Thomson in the mail by four. She had written a note to thank them for sending the information and to let them know that the Hannah mentioned in the letters was probably the same one in their family tree. She asked if they knew when she had died and how, hoping they would have the answer. She said she understood they did not travel much anymore, but Marilee invited them to come to Loyalist House for a few days as their guests. They would have much to talk about. She could arrange for Phillip to pick them up at the train station if that was a good way for them to travel. Maybe, by the time they received the letter and replied, she would have an answer about Hannah.

Walking on the main street of Newbrook was never a quick trip. Marilee always met friends, and invariably, a conversation would ensue about something happening at the museum or about new information for B&B owners. Today, she met Mary who had heard from Jeannie about the suspected ghost in their attic. Marilee worried that if this news spread too far, they might not have any guests wanting to stay at Loyalist House. She and Mary decided to go for coffee and chatted almost an hour. Mary was very interested and confessed that she had really wanted to somehow have the stately lady living in their garage leave to a happier place, but Joe wasn't so sure. She asked if she could come over tomorrow when Jeannie was coming to look at the letters. Marilee did not want this to turn into a circus and hoped that Jeannie had not told anyone else. She asked Mary to come at ten the next morning but not to tell anyone else about the meeting. Marilee decided she needed to go home before she met another friend.

Marilee arrived home to find Phillip in the kitchen, mixing drinks obviously for more than just him. He said friends he had met were here to talk about an investing opportunity. Marilee didn't know he was even contemplating investing in anything. She joined them on the patio and was introduced to Dave and Mike. Apparently they knew about some property that was about to be sold directly across from the B&B. It would be perfect for grapes, and it was large enough to qualify as a cottage winery. Marilee did know that Phillip had talked about setting up a winery, but she had thought it was a long-range plan. Mike and Dave had some winery experience, and as they had grown up in the area, they knew everyone. Being an accountant, Phillip certainly had a needed skill as well. Today, they were setting a fair price to pay for the land and then would contact the real estate agents and try to make a deal. Marilee was already jumping ahead and wondered what the winery would be called. She was pleasantly surprised when they told her it would be affiliated with the B&B and be called Loyalist

House B&B and Winery. She was thrilled, and now she had a new idea to keep her busy. She also really wanted to solve the present mystery in the house before starting on another project, especially with season two upon them. Marilee excused herself and went to the kitchen to start dinner. Now, her mind was really going a mile a minute. She decided it would just be simple hamburgers on the BBQ tonight with fresh asparagus as she couldn't think seriously about preparing food right now. During dinner, she and Phillip talked excitedly about all the events they could offer to their B&B guests, ranging from a tea room to special dinners to wedding receptions. Marilee did think that maybe they were getting too excited. After all, this was supposed to be a retirement project rather than three or four full-time jobs. Marilee was ready for bed that night even though she still had a bunch of ideas running through her mind. But just as she was drifting off, she heard once more the weeping of several people and saw them standing by the river in the morning mist.

Soldiers on the River

Hannah was so excited about the possibility of seeing Peter tonight she could not eat her dinner. Her mother noticed and asked Hannah if she was feeling fine. Hannah told her she had eaten a lot of berries while helping make the pie for dessert, and she was fine, just not hungry. Fortunately, her mother believed her, and so, after Hannah helped clean up the dishes, she was allowed to spend some time reading in her room before bed. Hannah, of course, took the latest letter from Peter and reread it several times. Just before her bedtime, she replaced the letter inside the doll, sewed around the neck again, and neatly wrapped the velvet ribbon around the neck to hide the stitches. She then decided that instead of wearing her brother's old clothes, she would wear something nice. She took her brother's clothes and wrapped the pants around the doll. There was really not a good place to hide this precious package in her room, so she tiptoed to the attic and put the doll in the bottom of the trunk. To hide it further, she placed a blanket on top of the doll and then replaced the linens that were already inside. No one would find them now. Hannah carefully returned to her room and began to decide what she would wear tonight. She knew it should be dark and not too long so as to cause her to trip, so she decided on a navy paisley printed dress of the empire style. The skirt was not too full, so she could lift it easily to step over roots and rocks. She would use her dark winter shawl to cover her head and shoulders while she waited by the river. Now she just had to wait until midnight. She hid the clothes under her covers so she could dress in bed when it was time to leave. Hannah was in bed wearing her night clothes when her mother came in to say goodnight. Her mother didn't seem to notice anything strange and, fortunately, did not feel Hannah's pulse, or she would have been concerned as it was racing. Hannah listened carefully until she heard the grandfather clock strike eleven thirty. It was difficult to put on stockings, a petticoat, and a dress while lying down, but Hannah managed it and sat on the edge of the bed to brush her hair and put on her slippers. Instead of wearing it in her locket, she took the coin Peter had sent her and put it in her pocket.

She stepped carefully as she knew where every creaky board was between the bedroom and the back door, and finally she was out of the house. The moon was not quite full anymore, but it was still bright enough to see the path to the river. A slight breeze was blowing, and Hannah now realized how thin the fabric of her dress was. She was glad to have her shawl pulled tightly around her. She crept down to her hiding spot and crouched down as best she could in her dress. Boys clothes really were better for these types of adventures. She took the coin from her pocket and held it in her hand. Just feeling the coin made her feel safer and closer to Peter. She listened carefully for any noise on the water, and it seemed like forever before she heard something. It was definitely the sound of someone paddling a boat or canoe in the river. Just as she stood up to whistle, the sound of guns firing rang in her ears. Hannah went to the water's edge and whistled to warn Peter, but the guns fired again. This time, Hannah tried to call out, but felt she had no energy to speak and could feel a stinging sensation in her neck. She very slowly fell off the dock into the water and disappeared.

By this time, there were several boats right at the dock, and the guns from boats on the river were still firing but seemed to be retreating back down the river. Two soldiers jumped onto the dock, but all they found was a shawl. They followed the path to the house as they were sure they had seen someone on the dock. Mr. Van Every was awakened by the gunfire and was downstairs collecting his gun when the soldiers banged on the door. He let them in and lit some lamps. They showed him the shawl and demanded to know whose it was and to wake everyone in the house as they would be searching the house to find out who the traitor was. Hannah's mother had gone to each of the children's rooms to wake the children and was alarmed to find Hannah's room empty. She did notice her nightclothes were on the bed. When she went downstairs, she told her husband quietly that Hannah was missing. Everyone else was accounted for, but when Mrs. Van Every saw Hannah's shawl, she began to weep. She knew her daughter was smitten with Peter Gillham but had been unaware they were meeting secretly. She also knew that if the British discovered Peter was secretly coming across the river, he would be sought out and killed as a traitor. She had always liked Peter, so she said nothing.

The soldiers searched through the house and found nothing but said they would wait until daylight to search the property. Fortunately, Mr. Van Every was well-known in the area as a loyal British supporter, so the soldiers did not suspect him of hiding a traitor. Mrs. Van Every took all the children back to one room and tried to calm them and get them back to sleep. Hannah's older brother seemed to know something was wrong and that Hannah might be involved, but he said nothing and just sat in bed in the dark.

When daylight came, the soldiers began searching the property. Hannah's mother and father followed the soldiers to the river, hoping not to find anything. The current was fast in the river, but the shoreline was covered with thick shrubs and trees growing out into the water. Just a few feet from the dock, there was something dark caught in the trees. When it was pulled back to the dock, to the horror of everyone present, they discovered it was the body of a young girl in a dark dress.

* * *

Marilee awoke holding her breath and was aware she had tears in her eyes. How could that have happened? Where was Peter? Now she knew what had happened to Hannah, but she was not happy about it. Marilee had wanted it to turn out differently. She looked at the clock, and it was 5:30 a.m., but she might as well get up as she'd never get back to sleep now. A pot of coffee would help, and she could get the letters in order for the meeting today. She really saw no need for a meeting as she felt as though she had lost a best friend. When Phillip came down for breakfast, Marilee told him the whole story. He was amazed that Marilee could dream about stuff that really happened and wondered if she could foretell the future of building a winery.

At ten, Jeannie and Mary arrived and immediately saw how sad Marilee looked. They all went into the dining room, and Marilee told them about the dream. At first, Mary didn't understand, but then they filled her in on how Marilee's dreams seemed to give all the answers to their questions about odd things that happened in the house. They sorted the letters in order, and they all were feeling very sad now that they knew what had happened to Hannah. Even two hundred years ago, young lovers would risk everything to be together. Not much had changed. Marilee felt it would be proper to donate the letters and the doll and the clothes to the museum as it was the history of this area. They all agreed.

Marilee also told Jeannie and Mary about finding a coin near the rhubarb bushes down by the river. This must have been the coin that Peter had given to Hannah. Unfortunately, it had not kept her safe.

Jeannie suddenly asked what they would do now that they knew there was a ghost in their attic. Marilee had not thought about that. Mary, who had been very quiet, suggested hiring Manfred back and having him release her to a better place, and at the same time, he could release the lady from their garage. Marilee would have to think about that and weigh the pros and cons of having a haunted B&B. It just might be another added feature to draw guests to Loyalist House.

Several days later, Marilee began to think about Hannah and why she had remained in the home all these years. Was she waiting for Peter to return? Was it the same Peter who had married her sister? Wouldn't it be better to be able to release Hannah from her earthly misery even though it could never be a happy release?

Marilee also decided to do some research on the internet to discover how people felt visiting and inhabiting haunted buildings. She found the results were mixed, but only people with a certain personality type were receptive to staying in haunted homes. There were also cultural opinions about homes where people had died or had resident spirits. If they ever wanted to sell their home as a B&B or a private home, they would have to declare to potential buyers the possibility that spirits lived in the attic.

There were a lot of decisions to make, and they could impact their business. Marilee and Phillip spent a lot of time discussing the pros and cons of hiring Manfred to release Hannah and, in the end, decided it was only fair to Hannah to release her spirit to a better place. Marilee would contact Manfred and ask him to come to Loyalist House to help them. She would also mention Mary's garage and the lady in the car. About three weeks later, she received a letter from Manfred, stating he would be pleased to help but was travelling in Tibet until late September. He would contact her when he returned, and they would set a date.

Marilee immediately told Jeannie and Mary. They were all amazed at Manfred's schedule and just hoped he would return from his travels. This would be a long summer waiting for his visit. It was decided by all that there would be no mention of Hannah's presence in the attic to the guests at Loyalist House.

Marilee reflected back on all that had happened during the past year. She and Phillip had purchased a house based solely on its suitability as a B&B and had ended up learning about life in a community two hundred years ago. Wars such as that one in 1812 still happened today because of disputes over land. Young lovers and families were still torn apart by a difference of beliefs and loyalties.

The future of Loyalist House had many unanswered questions, but the biggest one in Marilee's mind was: would she continue to have dreams in the mist?

WINDSONG'S FAVORITE RECIPES

Cheddar Tarragon Scones

These were a favorite at Windsong B&B, and we rarely had leftovers. There are two secrets to making light and fluffy scones:

1. Use buttermilk to make them tender.
2. Use grated frozen butter, which allows the water in the butter to remain separate from the flour by bursting into steam in the oven and helps the biscuits rise.

Ingredients

*2 cups all-purpose flour
*1 tbsp. baking powder
*½ tsp. salt
*1 tsp. dried tarragon
*½ C. frozen butter, grated, put into ½ cup section before freezing.
*1 egg, beaten
*3/4 C. buttermilk
*1/4 C. each of cheddar cheese and parmesan cheese

Method

1. Prepare pan using ungreased cookie sheet or line a cookie sheet with a silicone mat. Preheat oven to 350 degrees F.
2. Measure buttermilk into large measuring cup, add beaten egg, and mix together. Set aside.
3. Mix dry ingredients together, including the cheese, and stir with a whisk to incorporate air.
4. Just before using, grate butter on the large holes of grater into flour mixture, toss gently using fingers.
5. Add buttermilk mixture to flour and stir with the handle of a wooden spoon or a spurtle (used in Scotland to stir porridge). Stir only until the dough comes together and then use hands to form it into a ball. You can pat it lightly on a floured board and put it onto a pan and score it into 8 or 10 triangles, you

can roll it out and cut with a round cookie cutter, or you can drop it by spoonfuls onto the pan.

6. Bake at 350 degrees F for fifteen to eighteen minutes. Remove to a cooling rack.

7. Store in an airtight container.

8. These can be made the day before and reheated in foil at 350 degrees F for eight to ten minutes in the morning as the rest of the meal is cooking in the oven.

9. This recipe freezes well.

Variation

Instead of tarragon and cheese,

1. Add ½ tsp. lemon zest and ½C. dried sour cherries.
   Or

2. Add ½tsp. orange zest and ½ C. dried cranberries.

Baked Peach French Toast

This breakfast entree can be prepared the night before and refrigerated overnight. Fresh peaches from a local farm market make this dish very tasty.

Ingredients

* 1 loaf of Italian bread sliced in 1" slices (a day old is better than fresh). Allow 2 slices/person
*6 large eggs
*1 ½ cups milk homogenized or light cream
*5 tbsp. of peach preserves
*5 large ripe peaches peeled and sliced. Use fresh fruit or orange juice to keep peaches from turning brown
*½ cup toasted almonds
*Maple syrup
*Confectioners' sugar
*½teaspoon of almond extract (optional)

Method

Whisk together the eggs and peach preserves in a med. size bowl. Add the milk or cream and beat well. Slice bread and then cut each slice in half and place in a well-greased 9 × 13" baking dish in a single layer. You may need more than one pan depending on how many you are serving. Pour egg/milk mixture over bread until bread is covered with mixture. Cover baking dishes with plastic wrap and place in refrigerator overnight or at least a few hours.

Preheat oven to 350 degrees F. Bake French toast in oven for twenty-five to thirty minutes or until lightly browned on top.

Serve two half slices of the French toast on a plate, overlapping top with sliced peaches and maple syrup. Sprinkle with confectioners' sugar and toasted almonds.

We always served this with peameal bacon beside the French toast, but the French toast alone is a wonderful breakfast. Be sure to have this recipe for guests as they will always ask.

This recipe can be varied to accommodate any fruit in season. At Windsong B&B, we used strawberries in June, raspberries and cherries and blueberries in July and August, and apples in the fall and winter months. Note: When using red and blue fruits, remember to use apple jelly rather than preserves to match the fruit as the toast will turn an unappetizing purple color.

Twice Baked Individual Cheese Souffles

These are a great breakfast entrée as they can be made the night before and then baked again in the morning.

Ingredients

*10 oz. of partly skimmed milk
*3tbsp. chopped green onion
*2T. flour + 1tbsp. cornmeal
*½C. Cheddar cheese
*5 oz. of light cream
*1tbsp. butter cut into small pieces
*1/4 tsp. dry mustard
* 3 tbsp. grated Swiss or Gruyere cheese
*1tbsp. butter
*3 eggs separated + 1 egg white
*salt and pepper to taste

Method

1. In a small pan, warm the milk and the green onion. Remove pan from heat when bubbles begin to form around the edge of the pan.
2. Melt the 1tbsp. butter in a large saucepan, remove from heat, and add flour and cornmeal and stir into butter. Strain the heated milk and pour into the large saucepan with flour mixture and return to heat. Whisk continuously until mixture comes to a boil. Remove from heat and scatter butter pieces over the surface. Cover and cool slightly.
3. Set oven temp to 350 degrees, and butter 8 small ramekins (4 or 5 oz.). Uncover the pan and stir in the butter, followed by the egg yolks, cheddar, mustard, and salt and pepper. In a large bowl, whisk or beat 4 egg whites until stiff. Using a spatula, stir 1tbsp. of the egg white into the cheese mixture

to loosen it. Add the remaining egg white all at once and fold in just until combined.

4. Divide the mixture among the soufflé dishes gently to avoid losing any volume. Place the dishes in a baking pan that allows warm water to come 3/4 up the side of the soufflé dishes. Bake twenty-five minutes or until they have lightly risen and are firm to the touch. Remove from the water bath and leave to cool. Cover and keep in refrigerator overnight.

5. In the morning, preheat oven to 400 degrees about ten minutes before breakfast is ready to be served. Return soufflé dishes to the warm water bath as before. Pour a small amount of cream into each dish and sprinkle with cheese. Bake for ten to fifteen minutes or until risen and golden brown. Lift out of pan and dry the bottom of the ramekin and serve it immediately on a plate with the rest of the breakfast.

We often served this with tomato wedges on Boston lettuce.

Easy Asparagus Frittata

All the chopping and measuring for this entrée can be done the night before, making the morning rush a bit more relaxing.

Ingredients

*8 oz of fresh asparagus
*½ tsp vegetable oil
*4 green onions chopped
*1 clove of garlic chopped
*1/4 cup of oil-packed sundried tomatoes drained on a paper towel and chopped
*1/4 tsp. each of salt and pepper
*1 C. shredded Gouda cheese
*½ C. shredded cheddar cheese
*8 large eggs
*½ C. fresh bread crumbs
*3 tbsp. milk
*2 tbsp. fresh basil, chopped
*½ C. of chopped red and green peppers

Method

1. In a nonstick or regular frying pan, heat oil over medium heat. Add onions, garlic, tomatoes, and peppers and half the salt and pepper. Cook for two minutes, stirring to prevent overcooking.
2. Snap ends off asparagus and cut into bite-size pieces. In a shallow pan with a small amount of water, cook for three minutes until tender crisp. Transfer to a greased 9" pie plate. Sprinkle with half the cheddar and Gouda cheese.
3. In a bowl, whisk together the eggs, bread crumbs, milk, basil, and remaining salt and pepper. Pour over the asparagus mixture and sprinkle with remaining cheeses.

4. Bake in the center of the oven at 350 degrees for twenty-five to thirty minutes or until the middle is set. Let it cool on a rack for five minutes before serving. Serves 6.

    Heritage tomato wedges sprinkled with finely chopped basil make an attractive addition to this entrée.

Eggs Benedict

This always impresses guests as everyone thinks it is a glamorous entrée, but here is an easy way to make this. I learned this trick from watching cooking shows on TV.

Equipment Needed

*frying pan
*slotted spoon
*large deep pan filled with ice water
*1 custard cup

Poached Eggs: Allow 2 eggs/person. Break each egg into a custard cup before slipping it into a pan of hot, not boiling, water. This allows you to check the egg, and the end result is better as well. Take the custard cup and tip the edge into the hot water, allowing the egg to slip into the pan. I only cook four at a time in a regular-sized frying pan. Gently spoon hot water over the top of the egg, allowing the top to cook as well. After about two minutes or when the white looks fairly firm, lift the egg with a slotted spoon and place it in the ice water bath. Continue until all the eggs are precooked. (This is how they prepare this dish for five hundred people in hotels.) When you are ready to serve, slip the egg for about 1 ½ minutes back into the hot water. Remove again with a slotted spoon, slightly dry it on a paper towel, and place it on the toasted English muffin topped with a slice of peameal bacon. Top with Hollandaise sauce and sprinkle some fresh chopped chives.

Never Fail Hollandaise Sauce

There are many recipes for Hollandaise sauce in cookbooks, and you may have a favorite. I have even used the dry packaged mixes and had success. The problem with Hollandaise sauce is that it tends to curdle and separate if it sits any length of time. By stirring in a small amount, maybe a tablespoon at a time, of almost-boiling water and whisking it briskly, the curdling disappears, and you once again have perfect sauce.

Easy Strata

At a B&B, there are always leftovers. What to do with these is a dilemma as wasting food just does not seem right. At Windsong, we often packaged up the leftovers and gave them to the guests, especially when they were leaving and had a long car ride ahead of them. There always seemed to be bread leftover from toast to croissants. Making strata as an entrée solved this problem.

Ingredients

*about 5 C. of day old bread or croissants cubed
*½ C. chopped green and/or red peppers
*3 green onions finely chopped
*4 or 5 fresh basil leaves chopped
*3/4C. chopped ham
*6 eggs
*1 ½ C. milk
* 1 C. shredded cheddar cheese
*1 C. grape or cherry tomatoes cut in half
*3 tbsp. olive oil
*½ tsp. each dried oregano and basil

Method

1. Grease a 9"× 13" pan and place cubed bread in bottom of pan.
2. Sprinkle in peppers, onions, basil leaves, ham, and half the cheese over top of the bread.
3. In a medium bowl, beat the eggs and milk until well-mixed and pour over the top of the bread mixture. Press the bread down into the milk to make sure it is wet. Cover and refrigerate overnight.
4. Place the cut tomatoes in a bowl and cover with oil and spices. Salt and pepper may be added. Stir to mix, cover and marinate in fridge overnight.

5. Remove strata from refrigerator at least thirty minutes before baking. Sprinkle marinated tomatoes on top of strata and sprinkle with remaining cheese.
6. Preheat oven to 350 degrees. Place in center of oven and bake for thirty-five to forty minutes or until a knife placed in the center comes out clean. Let it rest for five minutes before serving.

There are many variations to this recipe. This is a savory dish, but sweet ones can be made with raisin bread and maple syrup or apples and cinnamon.

Ham and Egg Cups

Ingredients

* 2 slices of black forest ham/cup, not too thin or not too thick. Must be bendable but not burnable
*1/4 C. chopped green onion
*1/ 4 C. chopped red and or green pepper
*1 egg/cup
*salt and pepper
*3 tbsp. shredded cheddar cheese/cup

Method

1. Spray custard cups or muffin pans with cooking spray to prevent sticking. Preheat oven to 375 degrees.
2. Trim rind from the ham and cut it in a circle large enough to fit into the custard cup and up the sides. Place 2 slices of ham in each custard cup. Sprinkle a tsp. of precooked green pepper and onion onto the ham. To precook the vegetables, place the chopped vegetables in a container in the microwave and cook according to machine instructions until tender crisp. Crack the egg into a separate bowl and slip each egg into the ham cup. Sprinkle with cheese.
3. Place custard cups onto a baking sheet and bake in the oven for fifteen to twenty minutes or until whites are set and yolks still slightly runny.
4. Let it sit a few minutes before serving. Using a short spatula, carefully remove the eggs from the custard cups onto the plate. Tomato wedges on lettuce make a nice addition.

   If you are serving vegetarians, instead of ham, take a slice of whole wheat bread, remove the crusts, and roll it with a rolling pin. This will make a delicious base to hold the egg. Guests were always curious as to how I was able to shape the ham and have it stay that way.

Rhubarb Pecan Gems

This is a recipe that was found in an old book belonging to my grandmother. I updated it and added pecans.

Ingredients

*½ C. margarine
*½ C. brown sugar
*1 egg
*½ C. all-purpose flour
*½ C. whole wheat flour
*1 tsp. cinnamon
*½ tsp. baking soda
*1 tsp. baking powder
*1/4 tsp. salt
*3/4 C. stewed (cooked) rhubarb
*grated peel of 1 orange
*½C. rolled oats
*½ C. chopped pecans

Method

1. Cream together margarine and brown sugar. Beat in the egg.
2. Add sifted dry ingredients to creamed mixture alternately with the rhubarb. Sprinkle on grated orange peel and oatmeal and then mix just to blend. Do not overmix or they will not rise.
3. Fill greased muffin pans 3/4 full. Bake in a preheated oven at 350 degrees for twenty minutes.

Variations

This is such a good basic recipe that several flavors can be made by just changing a few of the ingredients.

Pumpkin

Replace stewed rhubarb with canned pureed pumpkin, and add ½ tsp. of all spice and nutmeg. Sprinkle a few more pecans on the top to give a bit of a crunch.

Apple Cinnamon

Replace stewed rhubarb with homemade or commercial unsweetened applesauce. Add ½ tsp. nutmeg. Grate ½ an apple and sprinkle over top before baking.

Strawberry/Raspberry/Apple

Add 1/3 C. of one the above fruits, mashed, to 2/3 C. of applesauce and continue as above. This is a good way to use up leftover fruit the next day.

Christmas Bubble Coffee Cake

This has been a favorite for many years in our house at Christmas. My children still request it. I even adapted this to make it sugar-free for our son the year he developed type I diabetes.

Ingredients

*2 packages of frozen dough shaped in balls. If these are hard to find, I use any shape of frozen rolls
*1C. butter, melted
*½ C. brown sugar
*½ C. red and green maraschino cherries
*½ C. slivered almonds
*1 package of butterscotch instant pudding mix

Method

1. Pour half the melted butter into a Bundt pan and spread it into all the creases of the pan.
2. Place the dough balls evenly around the pan. Sprinkle in the cherries and almonds around the outside edges.
3. Sprinkle the pudding mix and the brown sugar over the dough balls. Pour the remainder of the melted butter over the mixture in the pan. Cover the pan with a clean tea towel and sit it in a warm spot overnight to allow the dough to rise.
4. In the morning, heat the oven to 375 degrees. Bake the coffee cake for thirty-five to forty minutes or until the top is browning and it has risen to the top of the pan.
5. When cooked, immediately turn it out of the pan onto a plate that is larger than the pan. Let it cool slightly, and pull apart balls from the cake.

Variations

To make a sugar-free version, replace the brown sugar with sugar-free maple syrup. Use a sugar-free instant pudding mix, and omit the maraschino cherries. Bake in a small pan for an individual coffee cake.

Poached Pears with Fruit or Fruit Sauce

This makes a lovely fruit course in the fall and winter when fresh fruit is not always available in abundance.

Ingredients

*1 fresh pear/person
*enough water in a pot to cover the pears
*1 C. white wine
*1 cinnamon stick and several cloves
*½ C. frozen raspberries or strawberries

Method

1. Peel the pears, remove the core, and cut into quarters. Place in the water and white wine, cinnamon sticks, and cloves. Bring to a gentle boil and simmer until tender. Remove with a slotted spoon and place in a bowl. Cover with plastic wrap and refrigerate overnight.
2. Puree fruit using a potato masher just until fruit is broken down. Place in a sieve and mash through using the back of a spoon. This removes the seeds. Sweeten to taste, and keep puree in fridge overnight.
3. Next morning, place several pear quarters on a plate, drizzle with fruit puree. Garnish with mint leaves.

Fruit and Yogurt Parfaits

This is an elegant fruit course that lets you use those parfait glasses and spoons that have been in your cupboard since the 70s or were given to you by an elderly aunt when she sold her house.

Ingredients

*2 cups of fruit, any kind, chopped or not depending on the size
*2 cups vanilla yogurt
*shredded coconut
*crumbled graham wafers

Method

1. Layer fruit, yogurt, coconut, and wafer crumbs alternately in each parfait class. Top with a raspberry or strawberry and a mint leaf. Place glass on a plate and rest a parfait spoon beside the glass.

    When guests see this retro dish, they will smile and begin a conversation about their uses.

SELECTED BIBLIOGRAPHY

Carnochan, Janet. *History of Niagara*. Bellville, Ontario: Mika Publishing, 1973.

Langgath, A. J. *Union 1812: The Americans Who Fought the Second War of Independence*. New York: Simon & Schuster, 2006.

McCrae, John M. *A Van Every Story*. Lakefield Ontario, 1989.

Merritt, Richard, Butler, Nancy, and Power, Michael (Eds.). *The Capital Years: Niagara on the Lake 1792-1796*. Toronto: Dundurn Press and Niagara Historical Society, 1991.